# Sky Lake
## Summer

# Sky Lake
## Summer

Peggy Dymond Leavey

Napoleon Publishing

Cover art: Alan Barnard

Napoleon Publishing
an Imprint of TransMedia Enterprises Inc.
Toronto, Ontario, Canada

Le Conseil des Arts du Canada depuis 1957 | The Canada Council for the Arts since 1957

We acknowledge the support of the Canada Council for the Arts for our publishing program

Printed in Canada
05 04 03 02 01 00     5 4 3

Canadian Cataloguing in Publication Data

Leavey, Peggy Dymond
      Sky Lake summer

ISBN 0-929141-64-4

I. Title

PS8573.E2358S59  1999   jC813' .54     C99-930230-2
PZ7.L42Sk  1999

For Sarah, Kate and Emma
Who know about outdoor adventure
And for the little ones,
Tyler, Alexis and Ben,
With love.

*Chapter* **1**

1930

The fire bell rang for hours that night. Flames leapt from the walls of the house on the rock, shooting up through the roof and into the sky. To the boy, frozen at a window on the opposite side of the lake, even the clouds over there were on fire. A flotilla of boats had gathered below the rock face, silhouettes in the eerie light, tossing on a lake flecked with gold.

There was nothing they could do, the men said later, shaking water from their raincoats as they gathered downstairs in his father's store. Shivering, the boy crouched on the stairs, listening to the rough sound of the men's voices, their coughing, watching the steam which rose from their hair and the way the tobacco smoke curled around the lamp on the ceiling. No way to reach the house, they said, no place to land. Even the dock had disappeared. High above them, the fire had raged, unabated.

"Dang fool place ever to build a house anyway," one of the would-be rescuers pronounced, and this was followed by mutters of agreement. The boy's mother, tight-lipped, dressed in her housecoat, moved among them, a tea towel clamped to the top of the coffee pot.

At daybreak, only a pall of smoke hung over the scene on the other side. By noon, even that was gone.

"But those people," the boy's mother wondered out loud. "Did those people get out?" No one seemed to know.

# 1998

When she got on the four o'clock bus for Sky Lake, Jane Covington had already made up her mind that she was not going to talk to anyone. Her bad mood, which resulted from another early morning argument with her mother, still hovered in the back of her mind like some dark-winged bird. Right up to the last minute she had hoped her mother would change her mind, and for a change let her spend the summer in the city.

"I don't see why Nell can't come here for once,

if you're that worried about her being alone," Jane had grumbled. "Besides, I really wanted to visit Dad this summer."

Mary Covington, who was fitting newly-washed pairs of socks, like so many dinner rolls into Jane's dresser drawer, had paused for a moment. "And is that convenient with your father?" she had asked, in that see-how-well-controlled-I-am tone of voice she used whenever the two of them talked about Dan, Mary's ex-husband.

Jane had fallen back on her bed, expelling air from her lungs loudly and looking up at the ceiling. "I don't know. He hasn't asked me yet, but I want to be here when he calls. And I won't be if I have to spend the whole summer up at Nell's."

"Oh, for heaven's sake, Jane!" Mary had sputtered. "It's not for the whole summer." She had wedged in the last pair of socks and slammed the drawer shut. "I said for the month of July."

Jane had closed her eyes.

When someone drifted onto the empty seat beside her on the bus, Jane deliberately opened her book, sneaking only a brief peek at the reflection in the window. The bus driver pushed the passenger's carry-on luggage onto the shelf over their heads and promised to let her know when they had reached Sky Lake. "This young lady's getting off there too," he said.

3

Shifting over towards the window, Jane took another look in the tinted glass. In spite of the heat of early July, the woman was dressed in something long and flowing, gauzy, with flowers and numerous scarves. Her voluminous hair, which was neither blonde nor white, floated around her head like soft clouds. It was hard to tell from the window how old she was. Older than Mary, who had turned forty last week; closer perhaps to the age of her grandmother, Nell. To Jane's relief the woman did not want to talk and settled her head against the back of the seat with a sigh.

Shortly, the bus left the heavy traffic of the four-lane highway behind and turned north, away from the acres of car dealerships with their fluttering neon pennants, and into the rolling countryside where farms stretched out on either side.

As the miles disappeared under the wheels of the bus, Jane felt her heavy mood gradually lifting. There would still be the month of August left when she got home. And remembering the freedom she enjoyed at Nell's cottage brought an involuntary smile to her lips. It wouldn't be so bad. At My Blue Heaven she could sleep late, read all day if she felt like it and swim whenever she wanted to, within reason. Or do absolutely nothing at all. And Nell never reminded her that she really should be watching what she ate. Why, she was still a growing girl!

"I dreamed about coming here last night." The voice beside her startled Jane. "I believe in dreams, don't you?" the woman asked, smiling expectantly.

"Not really," Jane admitted, closing her book but keeping one finger in it to mark her place. "I never really thought about it."

"Oh, yes," the woman continued, "I believe dreams are meant to connect us somehow. Connect us to some other person, some other time perhaps."

Jane thought about this for a moment. It was an intriguing idea.

"My name's Mimosa," the woman said, turning in her seat and offering Jane a slim, cool hand. "Mimosa Granger. But everyone just calls me Mim." Her voice was soft and lilting, reminding Jane of music, or water running over stones. Maybe the woman was some sort of mystic. She certainly looked the part, with her loose garments and long, delicate neck. And ever since she had taken the seat beside her, Jane had been aware of the fragrance of flowers in the air. Was it roses? Lilies-of-the-valley? Something delicate, spring-like.

Mim wanted to know all about Sky Lake, and Jane, who had spent part of every summer there since she was eight, found herself describing it with growing enthusiasm. "And just wait till you see the big rock," she promised. "It's so high, it's amazing."

"It all sounds quite lovely," Mim agreed when Jane finally wound down. Ms. Granger had inherited a piece of property on the lake and was going up to take a look at it. "And then, most likely, I'll arrange to sell it," she said, playing with the ends of one of her scarves. "I could have done everything from back home in Massachusetts, but seeing as it's summer and I'm not tied to a job anymore, or to my poor old mother, God rest her soul. Not that 'tied to' is the right word, but I did look after her all those years."

"We're lucky, I guess," said Jane. "My grandmother doesn't need looking after. 'Though Mom feels better knowing I'm with her for part of the summer. Nell, that's what we all call her, goes up to My Blue Heaven every year at the end of May, and she stays right through till late October."

"My Blue Heaven on Sky Lake," Mim smiled. "How quaint."

"It's named after a song my grandparents liked," said Jane.

The bus was traveling now through a varied landscape, rocky terrain dotted with white birch. There were low-lying swamps at either hand, filled with the skeletons of drowned trees and sudden glimpses of lakes in the distance. When the familiar procession of roadside stands that sold home-baked treats and promised blueberries in season began, Jane knew they were nearing their destination.

The bus made the final turn into the dusty parking lot at the Sky Lake Marina, and Jane spotted Nell right away. She was fanning herself with her straw hat and talking to the boy who was filling her car with gas. Nell talked to everyone.

"She's got her car," Jane said, waiting for Mim to gather her floating scarves and get to her feet. "We can give you a ride to the place you're staying."

Once they were on solid ground, the driver cranked the door shut, and the three stepped clear of the fumes as the bus lumbered off. Jane introduced her grandmother to Mimosa Granger, Nell repeating Jane's invitation of a lift to her accommodations.

Mim eyed Nell's car with trepidation. It had so many dents and scrapes, such an accumulation of dirt, that it was hard to say what colour it had been. Mud colour, kind of. There were bits of loose chrome and rusted metal hanging off it everywhere, making it a challenge to get into it without tearing something. Nell called it the Lake Car. Back home in the city she used public transit.

"It's really no bother at all, Miss Granger," Nell insisted, misinterpreting Mim's hesitancy. "We go right past the Bide-a-Wee cabins."

Having no alternative, unless she wanted to wait for a taxi to come from the village out on the highway, Mim climbed into the back seat and sat with her bag clutched in both hands. They took off in a cloud of yellow dust, fishtailing their way to the top of the hill, Nell practically standing on the accelerator in order to force the car though the fresh gravel on the road. When they had crested the hill and started down the other side, Nell gave Jane a satisfied smile.

They dropped Mim off at the tourist cabins, and Nell refused to pull out of the driveway until Mim's wave from the door of the office indicated that her cabin was indeed ready.

Then began the final ascent, the road climbing above the roofs of cottages, the waters of Sky Lake dropping further below them on the left. It was all so familiar, it was like coming home. Jane smiled to herself, remembering the first time she'd come to Nell's summer place, how she'd wakened one night to the sound of music and had discovered her grandmother downstairs, dancing, swirling to the music, the hem of her skirt in either hand, a look of utter happiness on her face.

After witnessing that, Jane would amuse the two of them by inventing exotic past-lives for her grandmother. Surely, Nell Van Tassell had been a famous ballerina who had fled to this country to escape a corrupt government, or was the widow of exiled royalty, or a gypsy princess, even. In truth, she was just Nell, the widow of a man who used to sell farm equipment, but someone who had always been there for Jane.

"You still dancing, Nell?" Jane asked. Afternoon sunlight flickered through the trees as they passed.

"Every time the spirit moves me," Nell replied, gripping the steering wheel in front of her narrow chest and concentrating on the next curve in the road.

My Blue Heaven was at the end of the road. Just when Jane was sure the car was about to go slamming into the black and yellow checkered sign on the rock dead ahead, Nell yanked on the wheel and whipped the car to the left, coming to an abrupt halt at the back door of the cottage.

"We're here!" Nell announced, adjusting her hat back onto her head and looking as surprised as Jane to have survived the journey. And then, "Oh, I'm so glad you came, Janey." She put a hand on the back of Jane's neck and pulled her close.

"Didn't you think I would?"

"Well, I know how it is with teenagers. And you

turned thirteen this year, didn't you? I wouldn't have been surprised if you had decided to stay home with your friends."

"You know me better than anyone," Jane admitted, undoing her seat belt and trying in vain to get it to rewind. "Actually, Mom and I did have a fight about it. But now that I'm here, I know I'd miss this place if I didn't come for at least part of the summer. And you too, of course." Jane planted a kiss on the soft cheek before reaching for her knapsack.

Stepping out of the car, she was met by a familiar scent, the fragrance of warm grass and wild daisies, the earthy smell of moss and trees and old wood. She took a deep breath and was truly glad to be back. "Come on," she said. "I want to check things out. See what you've been up to while I've been gone."

Among the rituals the two of them performed each summer, putting the dock into the water was usually the first. Together they would wheel it down to the shore, digging in their heels to hold it back against the incline, and then finally heaving it out so that it met the water with a tremendous smack.

This year it was already in place, the old row boat tied to one of the rusty pipes at the end. Jane dropped the knapsack by the back door and jog-trotted down the slope to make sure she wasn't seeing things.

"You didn't wheel that dock down here all by yourself, did you?"

"Oh, no," Nell assured her as the two of them stepped onto the bleached boards, which rocked and bobbed under their weight. "I've got the nicest young fellow helping me out with odd jobs this year. All I have to do is let him know I need a hand, and over he comes in his boat. Jesse's a lovely boy."

Nell had never needed anyone to do odd jobs before, and that caused Jane to look a little more closely at the small woman beside her. "You feeling all right, Grandma?" she asked. The clear blue eyes still held the same sparkle, the pale skin under the braided crown of white hair didn't look any different. She had never thought much about Nell getting older, and she wasn't sure she liked the idea of some stranger doing the things she used to do for her.

"I'm perfectly fine, dear heart," said Nell. "And thank you for asking. Now, let's go up. I made us some lemonade before I went to fetch you."

My Blue Heaven was long past needing a coat of paint, being now more silver than blue. It seemed to Jane that every year it settled more comfortably into its surroundings. The rocks, with their embroidery of lichen, nestled against its stout foundation, and the feathery pines spread their branches to draw it more closely under their shelter.

A screened-in porch extended around the front and east side of the cottage. It was more like an outdoor living room, a shady space filled with small tables, piles of ancient books and magazines, mismatched lamps and pieces of old wicker furniture with fraying cushions. It had a throat-biting, musty smell to it. On days when the wind drew cool rain up from the lake, they could close the French doors to the porch and keep the bad weather out.

\* \* \*

Jane awoke on her first morning at Sky Lake to find sunlight flooding her upstairs room. From below came the comforting sounds of her grandmother moving about, closing windows against the chill of the new morning, lifting the lids of the cookstove. Jane snuggled deeper into the bed again, pulling the comforter up to her ears. Nell, she knew, would be making breakfast—oatmeal porridge with lots of brown sugar, a stack of golden toast, and fruit jam made right there in the kitchen of My Blue Heaven.

Downstairs, the phone was ringing. Throwing off

the bed covers, Jane dragged a pair of sweat pants and a shirt out of her knapsack, knowing it wouldn't be long before she could exchange it for shorts and a T-shirt. She pulled the brush through her thick, blonde hair and thudded down the stairs and into the kitchen. The oatmeal was erupting in little volcanoes in a battered pot on the back of the stove.

Mrs. McPherson, the egg lady, had called to remind Nell that she had three dozen brown eggs set aside for them. "I clean forgot when I went to fetch you yesterday," Nell said, handing Jane a knife to butter the toast.

They drove around the lake to pick up the eggs before noon, and Jane left the two women chatting in the pungent warmth of the McPhersons' back kitchen to tramp the short distance down to the marina store. The tinkle of the bell over the door announced her arrival.

She was the only customer, and the man behind the counter waited while she made her selection, then folded down the top of the small paper bag, leaving a pocket of air in the bottom with the raspberry jujubes—as though she'd bought a whole dollar's worth instead of just nine cents, the change she got back from the can of pop.

"Here for the holidays?" the shopkeeper asked, smiling.

Jane nodded, her mouth full of gummy candy.

"You're Mary Van Tassell's girl, aren't you? I haven't seen Mary in years. What's she up to these days?"

"My mother?" Jane's teeth had come unstuck. "She's selling real estate." She wasn't sure she should be telling this person these things. This tall, spare man with the thinning, foxy-coloured hair was not the shopkeeper she remembered from other summers.

"You say hi to your mother for me. Jackson Howard's the name. She'll remember."

"I'll tell her," said Jane, easing the door open.

She retraced her steps up the road, past the new municipal centre which had been under construction a year ago. A teenaged boy with a bandanna tied over his hair was crouched in the long grass, painting the lower part of the fence around the new building. His bare back was tanned from the sun. He stood up when Jane drew level with him and wiped the back of his neck with a paint rag. In his leather workboots, he was about the same height as she was, although she judged him to be a couple of years older. She had towered over most of the boys her own age since sixth grade.

"Hi," Jane said.

If he returned the greeting, Jane didn't hear

him. "There's a library in this building, isn't there?" she asked after a few awkward seconds.

"You can't take drinks in there," the boy said, a scowl spoiling his dark good looks.

"I wasn't going in now. Just wondering if they were open."

"At three," he said, and hunkered down again onto the tops of his boots, pulling the grass away from the fence and reaching for his brush.

There was no sign of activity up the road at McPherson's yet, so Jane followed the sidewalk around to the front of the building which faced the lake. Two long tables had been set up in the shade, and these were filled with old books for sale, showing various degrees of wear. She moved along one table where paperbacks had been set, spine side up, in long, ragged rows.

"Quarter apiece." The boy had come around from the other side.

"I'm just looking," Jane said.

"Well, I'm in charge," the boy informed her. "You want anything, just give the money to me."

Jane spent several minutes bent over the titles on the rows of spines in front of her. They were mostly old westerns or romances, nothing that interested her.

"What about these?" she asked, indicating some cartons underneath the table. She squatted on her heels and opened the flaps on one of the boxes.

"Hardcovers," said the boy. "Buck a piece. You Ms. Van Tassell's granddaughter?"

"That's right."

"She said you were coming this week."

"And you are?"

"Jess Howard."

Nell's handyman. "Hi," Jane said, trying the smile again. "I'm Jane Covington."

"I figured," the boy said.

Jane wondered if she might have red jujubes stuck to her front teeth. She drew one of the books out of the box, a small, blue volume with gold lettering on the cover. *The Sea and the Jungle*, by H. M. Tomlinson.

She flipped idly through it, knowing it too wasn't anything she'd want to buy, and wondered how long it would be before Jess Howard got tired of his surveillance. Suddenly, a piece of folded paper fell out of the pages of the book and fluttered onto the grass. She picked it up and unfolded it carefully. It was a handwritten letter and Jane read it, crouched over the carton of books.

"That's funny," she said as she stood up, frowning. "Look what was in this book."

Jesse's eyes passed quickly over it before he handed it back with a shrug.

General Delivery,
Sky Lake, Ontario, Canada.
September 7, 1930


Dear Madam:
I feel a bit of a fool asking you to help us. I'm afraid I don't even know your name. But you had such a kind face when you waited on me, and you smiled at my baby before we left your shop and got into the boat. I could think of no one else to turn to.

I think we may be in danger. My husband's brother is quite unwell. He has such terrible rages. I never would have come here had I known his true condition. I fear he may be losing his mind.

> Yours,
> Eugenie G. Fraser
> (Mrs. Thos. Fraser)


"Someone's old letter," remarked Jess.

"I know," said Jane. "But it's more than that. Whoever Eugenie G. Fraser is, she says she thinks she's in danger."

"So?" said Jess.

"Doesn't that bother you?"

Jess shrugged. "Not really."

"But it sounds like she's asking someone for help."

"Maybe you didn't notice the date," Jess suggested, with sarcasm.

Jane leaned her backside against the table and re-read the letter. The paper it was written on was very thin, its folds pressed flat by the book and the weight of the years. "It sounds as if she's afraid of her husband's brother. I wonder where it came from, who Eugenie G. Fraser is."

"By the return address, I'd say she was someone here on the lake," Jess said, picking paint from his fingernails.

"And this book must have belonged to the person who got the letter," Jane decided. "There's no envelope. I wonder who it was."

"The library gets donations like this all the time." Jess waved an all-encompassing arm over the rows of books. "Most of the time they're so old we can't use them."

"You work at the library?" Jane asked.

"Some of the time."

"Well, the letter was written to someone who ran a shop," Jane said, wrinkling her brow. "She says here, 'when you waited on me'."

"Could have been a waitress," suggested Jess.

"Then she wouldn't have said 'your shop'. She

says, 'when we left your shop' and 'before we got into the boat'. So it sounds like the shop was by some water. It could even have been the store right here at the marina."

"Could have been," Jess allowed.

"Do you know who ran the store in 1930?"

Jess shook his head. "No idea."

"I doubt if my grandmother would know either," Jane said, doing the math in her head. "In 1930, she would have been, oh, just little. Doesn't it make you the least bit curious about what happened to this poor woman?"

Jess's look was non-committal. "You can't just go and knock on her door after 68 years," he said. "'Hello Ma'am, are you still looking for help?'"

Jane decided to ignore the obvious. "We couldn't find out which house she lived in anyway," she pointed out. "General delivery means she picked up her mail at the post office."

Jess scratched the back of his neck and shifted his weight restlessly. "It's just an old letter. Probably someone was using it as a bookmark."

"Maybe," said Jane. He could be right. Perhaps she was making too much of it. "Look," she decided. "I've got to go anyhow. My grandmother will be waiting for me. Maybe you should just give this to the librarian. We probably shouldn't even have read it."

"Whatever," said Jess. Taking the folded paper from Jane, he poked it down into the pocket of his jeans. He followed her back around to the other side and bent to pick up his paint brush again.

"Nice to have met you," said Jane. She didn't expect a reply and didn't get one. She could see Nell getting into her car at McPherson's, and she quickened her pace before the vehicle came lurching down to meet her, spitting gravel and coughing dust onto the fresh paint.

She needn't have worried. The Lake Car stalled before it reached the end of the driveway, and Jane seized the opportunity to clamber inside.

"I see you met young Jesse," Nell smiled, gears grinding as they took off.

Jane opened the bag of candy and held it in Nell's direction. "Do you know anyone named Fraser around here?" she asked.

Nell shook her head and waved the candy away. "Can't say as I do. What did you think of Jesse Howard?"

"Weird name for a boy, if you ask me."

"Not at all. It's Biblical, in fact. Nice-looking young man, don't you think?"

Nell's car was awfully hot and the window on Jane's side didn't roll down any longer. "He's okay," Jane said. "Not exactly what I'd call friendly. Oh, the man at the store said to say hi to Mom."

"Jackson Howard," Nell nodded. "Man with his name on backwards."

Jane blew into the empty bag and, holding it shut, burst it with a bang. "So you never heard of anyone named Fraser? Mrs. Thos. Fraser?"

"Why?" Nell asked, affording her a quick glance. "What's this all about?"

"There was a book sale at the municipal centre," Jane explained. "I was looking at some of the old books and a letter fell out of one of them. It was all folded up, from someone called Mrs. Thos. Fraser, and it was written in 1930."

"Long time ago," said Nell, craning forward to negotiate a curve in the road.

"I know, but the weird thing about this letter was that this Mrs. Thos. Fraser said she thought she was in danger, and she was writing to someone, asking for help."

"What kind of danger?"

"I don't know for sure. She said her husband's brother had 'terrible rages'. That she never would have come if she'd known."

"My word! That does sound ominous," Nell agreed.

"It was written to a woman who looked after a store, and the store was somewhere near water. I figured out that much. Maybe even the store here at the marina."

"I'm not sure who would have had the store here, way back then," said Nell. "It's nice to see the Howards take it over now, though. Jackson's been out west for years. He and Jesse came back just last fall."

"Then Jess is his son?"

"That's right."

Jane looked at her watch, relieved that there would still be time for a swim before lunch. "I wonder what happened to Mrs. Thos. Fraser," she mused, picking up one of the warm brown eggs which nestled in the container on the seat between them.

"Thos. is short for Thomas," said Nell. "Mrs. Thomas Fraser."

"Whatever," said Jane, holding the egg to her cheek. "I'll just call her Eugenie."

# Chapter 2

A steady rain greeted Jane her second morning at the cottage. All day it drifted, ghostlike, back and forth across the lake and sighed through the dismal trees. Jane spent most of the time reading, curled up under the lamp on one of the couches in the living room, listening to the rhythmic creak of Nell's rocking chair, the intermittent popping of the fire in the cookstove, eventually falling asleep. When she awoke, stiff and chilled, she went to draw a chair up in the warmth of the kitchen where her grandmother was playing solitaire.

"I expect you needed that nap," Nell said when Jane apologized for dropping off.

"Mom says I sleep too much," Jane yawned. "She dragged me to the doctor, but I could have told her I wasn't sick. Maybe I sleep to avoid arguing with her."

"That's too bad," said Nell, counting out three

more cards from the pile she held in her hand. "I expect it's a stage you're both going through."

Jane stood up and stretched her arms above her head. "Mom doesn't try to understand me anymore," she stated flatly.

"Do you do the same for her?" asked Nell, looking up from the cards on the table.

"What's to understand?"

"She hasn't had an easy life, Jane."

"Oh, you mean because of Dad? She's the one who sent him away."

Jane saw Nell bite her lip. "I think you know better, dear."

Jane pretended to concentrate on the length of spider web strung between the little china figurines on the window sill, separating them one by one from its clutch. The worst thing she had ever heard Nell say about Dan Covington was that he was a man of little strength. 'Though Jane never knew what staying at a nine-to-five job had to do with a man's strength. To Jane, her father was a man who dreamed dreams, a man who felt he had to follow them. Always sure that the next get-rich-quick scheme was the one that would do it for him, he had come and gone many times during Jane's childhood, until finally Mary had suggested he leave altogether. But no one had ever bothered to ask Jane how she felt about it.

*     *     *

She is running, her mouth gasping for air, her legs pumping wildly. Her arms ache with the weight she is carrying. But no matter how hard she runs, she is slowly being drawn back towards a swirling vortex, back towards whatever it is that she is fleeing.

Jane awoke suddenly and sat up with a gasp, her pulse pounding. She had been dreaming. Realizing that was all it was, she lay down again, only to resume the tossing she'd started before the nightmare. She shouldn't have spent so much time sleeping during the day, she decided. What was it the woman on the bus had said? That dreams are meant to connect you to something? She tried to recall the dream, to put together the pieces and think about what she might have been running from.

She was eating her cereal at the kitchen table the next morning, her book propped open in front of her, when Nell came back inside from the clothesline.

"Will you look at this?" Nell sounded exasperated. She set what looked like an ordinary red brick on top of the wood box inside the back door. "It's not the first one to fall off the chimney. I absolutely must get some mortar and get it repaired." She was already at the telephone, pressing buttons.

"Morning, Jackson. It's Nell Van Tassell. Oh, fine, fine. Looks like a grand day. Yesterday's rain was just what we needed."

Jane closed her book and took her breakfast dishes to the sink. How hard was it to put two bricks back on a chimney anyway, she wondered? Outside, she discovered the day was warming up quickly. She swung herself into the old striped hammock which sagged between two poplar trees in the side yard, pushing herself off with one foot, swinging there, facing the lake where the sunlight glinted. She waited for Nell.

Today, they were going to take a picnic lunch and row over to the island, see what the crop of raspberries was going to be like this year. Of all the cottagers on the lake, Nell was the only one Jane knew who still considered a stout set of oars and muscles to match the best way to power a boat.

The screen door slammed and Nell came down the steps towards her. "It's all set then," she announced. "Jesse's picking up some supplies and he's going to fix the chimney for me. Right away. You don't mind having our picnic here, do you, dear? We use that stove everyday, and the chimney is dangerous the way it is."

Jane gave herself another push to set the hammock in motion again. "Jesse didn't mind coming?"

"Well, I didn't actually speak to him," Nell admitted, dropping her hands into the pockets on the front of her denim skirt. "But when I asked his father about getting some mortar, Jackson said he'd send Jesse over to do the work for me. He'll do some other little jobs while he's here. What teenager doesn't need a little extra money these days?"

Nell went back inside and Jane debated whether she should go for a swim first or putter about in the row boat for a while. The warmth of the sun was making her lazy. Maybe she would go and look for the raspberries herself. She would just as soon not be here when Jesse arrived, considering his surly attitude when they had first met. But she did wonder if he might have discovered anything more about the strange letter she'd found.

Jane had gone upstairs to straighten her room when she heard the sound of an outboard motor approaching. From the window, she saw Jess Howard pull his boat into the empty berth on the other side of the dock, get out, tie the boat to the pipe, and reach down for a paper sack, which he slung onto his shoulder. Then he strode with it up the incline to the cottage. The bandanna was gone from the dark hair, and he had added a white T-shirt to his wardrobe of jeans and workboots.

Jane heard Nell go out to greet him, and the sound of their voices moved around to the back. From the window at the head of the stairs, Jane watched as Jess entered the shed and came out with the ladder. He set it down on its side against the building. Reaching over his shoulder with one hand, she saw him pull his T-shirt off over his head and stuff it into the waist band at the back of his jeans. Then, before bending to pick up the ladder again, he looked directly up at the window. Jane stepped back quickly, feeling the colour rise in her face, knowing she'd been caught.

"Oh, there you are," said Nell when Jane came down into the kitchen again. "Could you take Jesse this lemonade, dear?"

"Oh, Nell. He just got here! Couldn't it wait?"

"It's pretty hot around there on the east side, Jane. Jesse will be here for a while. He's going to set the stones back in the front planters for me, do some other repairs. It wouldn't hurt you to be a little more friendly, would it?"

"He didn't act like he was looking for a friend," Jane said. She took the glass without another word and found Jess on the far side of the cottage, mixing mortar in the old wheelbarrow. She wished now that Nell hadn't made that remark about his looks the other day, and she especially wished that he hadn't seen her watching him from the window on the stairs.

"My grandmother sent you some lemonade."

"Thanks," said Jess, without raising his head.

"Could I set it somewhere?"

"I'll take it." He reached for the dripping glass and downed it all at once.

Jane stepped carefully over the coil of hose to stand in the shade of the lilac bush. "Working hard?" she asked, realizing as soon as the words were out how lame they sounded.

"You bet," Jess said and handed her back the empty glass.

Might as well cut to the chase. "Did you find out anything about what we found on Tuesday?"

He paused for the briefest second, as if trying to remember Tuesday. "I know where that box of books came from, if that's what you mean."

"You do? All right!"

Jess shoved the tip of the shovel into the paper sack, carefully drawing out some powdery, white material and tossing it into the wheelbarrow. "Just like you figured," he said, "Sky Lake Variety Store, right there on the box. Didn't see it till I was putting it back inside last night."

Jane frowned. "They were your dad's books?"

"No. They were in boxes in the storeroom when

we took over. My dad gave them to the library."

"And the letter?" she pressed. "What did you do with it?"

"I've got it."

"You're still carrying it around? I thought you were going to give it to the librarian."

"I couldn't," Jess said. "She started her holidays this week. Her replacement wouldn't know anything about it."

"So? Did you show it to anyone else?"

"Like who?"

"I don't know." Didn't he have any imagination? "Your parents, maybe. Someone who might have known the Frasers."

Jess stirred the contents of the wheelbarrow. "I didn't show it to anyone."

"Oh," said Jane. "Maybe I should just let Nell see it, then."

"Go ahead. It's all yours." He set the shovel down and drew the letter out of the pocket of his jeans with two fingers.

Nell was in the kitchen washing lettuce, laying each leaf out on a clean tea towel she'd spread on the counter. At Jane's invitation, she sat down to read the letter which Jane unfolded for her on the kitchen table.

When she was through, Nell removed her glasses, shaking her head. "I agree. Whoever

Eugenie is, she sounds frightened."

"Sounded, you mean," Jane reminded her gloomily. "This letter is 68 years old."

"That's true. So whatever she was afraid was going to happen, either did, or didn't."

"We don't even know if the storekeeper was able to help her or not."

"Or if she ever got the letter," Nell added.

"Well, Jess just told me that the book came from the storeroom of his father's store," Jane pointed out. "So we know the letter got that far."

"There's really nothing you can do now, dear," Nell said kindly.

"Maybe not. But I'm still curious."

At lunchtime, at Nell's request, Jane carried a plate of chicken sandwiches covered with plastic wrap around to the side to Jess, only to discover he'd gone down to the dock. She found him dangling his legs in the water, his jeans rolled up to his knees.

"She didn't have to feed me," Jess growled when he saw the sandwiches, but accepted the plate Jane handed him anyway.

His dark hair curled up at the back of his neck, and he had missed a streak of white paint above the elbow of his right arm. Seeing the paint made Jane feel she had the advantage, that she knew something about him he didn't want her to know:

he wasn't nearly as tough as he thought he was. She walked on out and pretended to check the rope that held Nell's boat, wishing she could do it without making the dock bounce so much. She shouldn't have eaten that second piece of chocolate cake at supper last night.

"You swim off this dock?"

Jane turned back towards him. "Of course," she said.

"Drops off kind of fast, doesn't it?"

"This is the deepest side of the lake."

"And you must be one heck of a swimmer," said Jess.

"I am," said Jane, dragging her foot in the water and making a deliberate pattern with it on the dry planks of the dock. "And I learned to swim right here."

Swinging his legs out of the water, Jess rested the weight of his upper body behind him on his hands and squinted up at her. "Must be nice to be a rich kid and get to lie around the cottage all summer," he said.

It occurred to Jane that he was trying to start an argument. "A rich kid? Is that what you think I am?"

"Well, aren't you?"

"No, I'm not. And you know something? I think you have an attitude problem."

"So what's it to you?" he challenged.

"Nothing. But it must get in the way of making friends."

"So who said I needed friends?"

Jane glared at him. She had half a mind to give him a shove, send him sideways off the dock into the lake. "From the very first time you spoke to me, it was like you were looking for someone to fight with," she said. "What did I ever do to you? For your information, I started spending summers here the year my parents split up. My grandmother looked after me then, and now my mother counts on me to sort of keep an eye on her. Until you came along, I helped her with some of the heavy work too."

They seemed to have locked eyes in a furious stare, and to Jane's surprise, it was Jess who looked away first. "Don't sweat it," he muttered, and bent to work the legs of his jeans back down over his shins.

Jane turned to leave.

"Here, you forgot something." But when Jane reached for the empty plate he held towards her, he made a little gesture to jerk it back again. Jane gripped it firmly, with a sigh of exasperation.

"You really get steamed, don't you?" Jess said, as she turned from him. "Okay, so I have an attitude problem. Maybe I'm working on it."

"You need to." Without waiting for him to get

to his feet, Jane walked quickly back up to the cottage.

She spent the rest of the afternoon indoors, tidying the stacks of photo albums on the shelves in the living room, re-arranging the collection of battered duck decoys that circled the room, watching the top of Jess's head through the side window and wondering what it was that made him so angry.

Jane dropped by the kitchen later, where her grandmother was figuring out what she owed Jess for his afternoon's work. "So what d'you think his problem is, anyway?"

"His problem?"

"He's got a chip on his shoulder like you wouldn't believe."

Nell lowered her eyes to the scrap of paper on which she was writing. "Well, let me see. His mother died not too long ago. And he moved back here, half a continent away from where he grew up. Maybe that's it." Jane wasn't so sure.

\*    \*    \*

She was sitting on the dock, her towel wrapped around her after a swim, when Jess came back down to his boat about four o'clock. She had been watching two climbers scaling the massive wall of rock which dropped steeply into the lake, west of My Blue Heaven. The rock was a landmark on Sky Lake, the only feature to distinguish this lake from a thousand others nestled in the granite landscape of the Canadian Shield.

"You ever been up to the top?" Jess asked, shading his eyes to look in the same direction.

That he even spoke to her surprised Jane, let alone that he had initiated the conversation. "No, have you?" she asked.

"Sure. All the kids around here have." So he just wanted to brag. He bent to untie the rope which held the boat to the iron pipe.

"You must have some pretty good mountain climbers around here then," Jane said, matching Jess's earlier tone. For an instant, he looked as though he might even smile.

"Oh, they don't go up the hard way," Jess admitted. "Only the real climbers go up the face of the rock. There's an easier way to the top, a trail hidden in a little cove on the other side. It's pretty steep, but at least it's not sheer rock." Dropping the rope into the boat, he held the vessel against the dock with his foot.

"So what's up there?" Jane asked.

"Not much. Foundation of an old house. But the view from up there is really cool. So long as you're not afraid of heights."

"I'm not," said Jane, amazed at the length of the conversation.

"You ought to get someone to show you where the trail is then," said Jess, stepping down into the boat.

Jane got to her feet, tucking her beach towel into itself across her chest. "Nice boat," she remarked. After what Nell had told her, she felt she should say something kind.

"Yeah, well, it's not mine. My dad lets me use it, but I can't mess around." Jess lowered the motor into the water. His eyes met hers briefly. "See you," he said, looking away.

Jane watched while Jess maneuvered the boat away from the dock, waiting to see if he'd turn and wave. He didn't, but it didn't seem to matter anymore. She found herself smiling, warmed by a feeling that it might be an okay summer after all.

✳   ✳   ✳

On Sunday night when the rates were low, Mary called to talk to Jane. "Wonderful news, Janey," she announced. "I asked Carol if Corrie would like to spend a few days up there with you, and she jumped at the chance. I guess, since this is the first summer she hasn't spent at camp, she must be feeling a little lost. I can't imagine why you didn't tell me Corrie would be home all summer."

When there was no response from Jane's end, Mary went on. "I understand how much you wanted to stay here this year, Jane, but since that wasn't possible, with my Open Houses and everything, maybe having Corrie there will be the next best thing. You're awfully quiet, Jane. Aren't you happy at the idea?"

"Sure, that's okay, Mom. I just thought you might have asked me first."

Jane remained on the bench under the telephone after the conversation was through. She was still sitting there, picking at the threads on her cutoff jeans, when Nell returned to the room.

"Problem?" she asked brightly.

"Just Mom," Jane sighed, looking up. "She makes all the decisions for me. Did you know about Corrie coming?"

"She asked me first," said Nell. "Isn't it a good idea?"

"It's not that, really. There's lots of stuff here I can show her, I guess." She chose her words with care. "Corrie really isn't used to cottage life, Nell."

"I thought you said she went to camp every summer."

"Not real camp, Nell. Riding camp. Where everyone stays in a lodge, with a dining room and a Jacuzzi and everything. Or computer camp. Where they all stay in the university residence."

"I see." Nell drew a carton of milk from the fridge and poured herself a glass, part of her bedtime routine.

"What really bothers me," Jane continued, "is that Mom never lets me make my own choices. She decides everything for me."

"She needs to let you grow up a little, you mean," said Nell. "Milk, dear?"

"Exactly," said Jane, taking the glass. "Do you know she has even decided I don't need to go and see my dad?"

"I think she's trying to spare you, dear. You didn't have a very good time the last time you visited him."

"I know. But maybe things are different now."

"Perhaps," said Nell quietly.

There seemed to be nothing more to say on that subject, and Jane clumped upstairs to lie on her bed a while, study the familiar brown stains on the ceiling and think about Corrie coming. Without even knowing it, Corrie could spoil everything.

It wasn't only that her friend wasn't used to lumpy mattresses or musty pillows or outdoor toilets. Certainly, she would never understand why Nell put up with the garter snake which chose to sun itself on the flat stone at the back door; or all the spiders, whose webs caught you by surprise and which you sometimes wore in your hair all day. Corrie would be totally grossed out. No, it wasn't only that. Now there was Jess.

*     *     *

Jane didn't have much to say on the trip around the lake on Tuesday to meet Corrie's bus. Nell took a hand off the wheel long enough to give Jane's knee a pat. "It'll be fine, dear," she promised. "You'll see."

Jane returned a weak smile. Back in the city, Corrie Ottley was Jane's closest friend. But that was at home; Sky Lake was different. Sky Lake belonged to her.

When Corrie stepped down off the bus, she looked like an ad for an outdoor store—new hiking boots, khaki shorts and matching blouse with barely a wrinkle, even after a long, hot ride. A gold clip held her hair off her face. Corrie's fine brown hair was perfectly straight and shone like silk. In contrast, Jane's blonde mane only got frizzier with the heat and humidity, and her clothes were rumpled and comfortable. After a week, most of them were still in her knapsack.

"I just didn't know what I was going to do till you got back, Jane," Corrie bubbled, letting Jane take one of her two matching suitcases. "I'm so glad you and Nell invited me."

"We're glad too, dear," said Nell warmly. "Now, I must warn you that My Blue Heaven doesn't have all the creature comforts. But as Jane and I always say, who needs them when we have nature right at our back door. Right, Janey?"

Jane slid the luggage onto the seat and ducked back out of the car. "Right, Nell," she said, thinking of the snake.

Before they headed back around the lake, there were supplies to pick up from the store. While Nell filled her basket and chatted with Jackson Howard, Corrie and Jane wandered around the big, airy room attached to the front of the building and Jane got caught up on news from the home front. She had already decided she was not going to ask Corrie how the party two nights before she left had turned out, the one Corrie had been invited to and she hadn't.

They were eating ice cream and studying the trophy fish mounted on the walls when Jesse came into the room. Seeing the girls, he stopped and took the broom he was carrying off his shoulder. "Oh, sorry," he said. "Didn't know there was anyone here."

"It's okay, isn't it?" Jane asked. "We were just looking around, waiting for my grandmother."

"No problem. My dad asked me to sweep the floor, is all. We had a bingo in here last night." He was staring at Corrie.

"Oh, Jess," said Jane quickly. "This is my friend, Corrie Ottley, from home. Corrie, this is Jess Howard. He lives here."

Corrie tucked a long strand of hair back behind her ear and turned on her brightest smile. "Hi, Jess," she said. She had mocha ice cream on her upper lip.

Jess leaned on the broom and continued to stare. This was exactly what Jane had been afraid of.

"You're so lucky to live in a place like this," chirped Corrie, indicating the view of Sky Lake and the rock on the opposite shore.

"He's one of the lucky ones who has a job, too," Jane pointed out. "Jess works at the municipal centre."

Jess gave a short laugh. "You wouldn't want that kind of job," he said.

"What's wrong with it?" Jane asked. "Isn't the pay any good?"

"The pay is zip. Zilch? Nada? I'm doing community service."

"That's nice," said Corrie, and before either one of them could ask him to explain, Nell suddenly scurried into the room. "Ooh, isn't it lovely and cool in here!" she cried. "Jane dear, no need to trouble Jesse about the groceries. I told Mr. Howard I had two big, strong girls to take them out to the car for me."

"Aren't you the sly one?" Corrie muttered as they loaded plastic bags into the trunk of the Lake Car.

"What do you mean?" asked Jane.

"Jess, of course. And you pretending you didn't want to come up here this summer."

The truth, Jane knew, wasn't half that interesting.

Corrie declined Nell's invitation to join them for a dip in Sky Lake that night, in spite of Jane's promise that it would be as warm as her bathtub at home. Corrie preferred to stay on shore, toasting marshmallows to golden perfection on the end of a stick, while Jane and her grandmother splashed in the moonlight and counted the other campfires around the lake.

\*　　\*　　\*

It was the next morning, after her breakfast was properly digested and Jane had given her a tour of Nell's property, that Corrie agreed to try the water. Jane bounded up the stairs, two at a time, and squirmed into her damp bathing suit, wishing she'd taken the time to hang it out on the line to dry, instead of over the back of the chair in her room. She felt like a whale beside Corrie in her pink bathing suit and dived off the dock as soon as she reached it.

Grasping the dock with one hand, Corrie hesitated before entering the water, balancing herself on the round stones, her upheld foot dabbling. "Do you suppose there are any things in this lake?" she asked worriedly.

"Like what?"

"Like snakes or fish or things that bite?" Already she had been attacked by black flies. When she'd put her hair up to go swimming, Jane had seen that there was a lot of blood on the back of Corrie's neck.

"Oh, Corrie, of course there are fish," Jane sputtered, treading water. "It's a lake! Don't be such a wuss."

"I think I'll just sit on the dock and watch you," Corrie decided, sitting down firmly and drawing her feet up underneath her. "I'm not really all that hot."

Jane didn't believe that for a minute. In exasperation, she struck out away from the dock with a determined, overhand crawl. Several metres out, she rolled onto her back and floated for a while. Then she swam in again.

Gripping the end of the dock, Jane let her legs flutter out behind her and watched Corrie examine her toenails. "You don't know what you're missing," she teased, but in a gentler tone.

Corrie gave her a wan smile and drew her knees up under her chin. How was it, Jane wondered, with all Corrie had going for her, that she could make Jane feel pity?

Jane boosted herself up onto the dock and plopped down beside her friend. "Last night, when we were talking, you never told me about the party. The one I missed?" She grimaced. "Okay, so I didn't miss it. I wasn't invited."

"There's not much to tell." Corrie rested her cheek on her knees, looking away.

"You went, didn't you?"

"I went."

"And Dillon? Was he there?"

Corrie took the elastic band out of her hair and shook it loose. "He was there. But I wish I hadn't been."

"Why not?"

"Because he's not interested in me. He made that obvious."

Jane stared at her. "How can you say that, Corrie? He made a point of asking you if you'd be there."

"You want to know the truth, Jane? I spent the night reading the liner notes on all the CDs, opening and closing the fridge for everyone else."

"That's usually my job," Jane said, ruefully.

"There wasn't a whole lot else I could do," Corrie admitted. "Dillon was there, but he was all over Tasha. And I mean all over."

Jane couldn't think of a single thing to say after that, but she understood Corrie's pain all too well.

At noon, after they had changed back into their clothes, the girls found Nell sitting in the sun porch, surrounded by photo albums. "Seeing you tidying all these albums the other day, Jane, reminded me that one of my projects this summer was to organize the rest of my pictures. I never knew I'd collected so many." She smiled up at them. "You two can fix yourselves some lunch, can't you? Whenever you're hungry?"

"No problem," agreed Jane, dropping into a chair and picking up one of the albums, a book of sepia-toned pictures which were attached to the pages with fancy little corner pieces.

"Do you know who all these people are?" Corrie wondered, sitting on the upholstered arm of Jane's chair.

"Not all of them, to be sure," replied Nell. "These books go back to when my parents first bought My Blue Heaven."

Over the years, the albums had changed from hefty books with soft, black paper, to three-ringed binders with pages of plastic pockets. All of them were filled with photographs of relatives and friends who had crowded up to My Blue Heaven in years gone by.

"Our visitors used to come by rail," Nell told them. "When the train still stopped here. I remember my parents would go to meet them at the station. Or they'd come by car with their luggage strapped to the roof for a long stay. There'd be so much company that at times there'd be two or three tents pitched on the flat place at the back of the cottage." She had pictures of just such a scene to show the girls.

The oldest of the photographs were grainy scenes of Sky Lake, of people sitting on blankets under the trees, men with their hair parted in the middle, wearing weird bathing suits with attached tops.

Some of the pictures had come unstuck from the pages of the album, and a handful of these had been tucked into the binding. Jane shuffled slowly through them and found one which was a view of the big rock, taken from offshore. She drew the photograph in for a closer look. Now that was odd. There was a house at the top of the rock.

She turned the picture over to read the handwriting on the back. "The Fraser place," it read.

"Oh, my gosh!"

"What, what?" demanded Corrie, craning to see.

Shoving the heavy album off her lap, onto the coffee table, Jane waved the picture at Nell. "The Fraser house, Nell! Look! Jess said there was the foundation of an old house on top of the rock."

"Well, yes, there was a house up there at one time." Nell took the picture and examined it herself. "Though never in my memory."

"But see what it says on the back! The Fraser place!"

"My word! So it does. Do you suppose that...?"

"It must be! That's where the letter must have come from! Eugenie G. Fraser must have lived up there in the house on the rock."

Corrie was looking from one to the other in bewilderment. "What letter? And who is Eugenie G. Fraser?"

"It's a long story," Jane told her, taking the picture over to the window and studying it again, struck by the fact that for the second time since she'd arrived she'd seen the Fraser name. The clock on the fireplace mantel sounded the hour.

"My goodness! One o'clock already," exclaimed Nell. "No wonder my tummy's rumbling. Why don't you go make us some sandwiches, Jane? And you can tell Corrie all about your Eugenie G. Fraser."

Corrie was walking up the back of Jane's heels as she trailed her into the kitchen, looking ready to burst with curiosity. While they buttered bread and sliced cheese together, Jane told her about the letter she had found, with its puzzling message.

"All the good stuff happens to you," grumbled Corrie, getting plates down out of the cupboard. "Haven't you ever noticed?"

Jane paused, knife poised over a ripe tomato and considered. "Well, I think you have an interesting life too," she said, feeling generous.

"No, I mean it," Corrie said. "My life just goes on its boring way, but you have all the excitement. Like the stuff with your dad, and getting to come here to Nell's every summer and having this Jess as your friend, and now this mysterious cry for help. From the past, no less. That kind of stuff never happens to me."

When she put it like that, Jane had to agree with her. Although the part about her dad had caused her more pain than excitement. That her life might be enviable put a whole new perspective on it. One she hadn't considered before.

Jane propped the picture against the milk jug on the table and continued to examine it while they ate their meal. The Fraser place had been a large, white frame house, with a central stone chimney and six tall pillars at the front supporting a full verandah. A closer inspection of the oldest albums failed to turn up any other pictures of the rock with the house at its pinnacle.

"So what happened to it, Nell?" Jane asked, reaching for an apple from the bowl in the middle of the table and polishing it on the front of her T-shirt.

"It burned down." Nell dunked a tea bag in and out of the hot water in her cup. "The way I remember the story, anyway. As I said, as far back as my memory goes, the rock looked the way it does today. Bare."

"Maybe someone really old would remember the house," Corrie suggested.

"Thank you, dear," Nell said sweetly.

When they went to bed that night, Jane lay awake a long time, her arms folded behind her head, listening to Corrie's soft breathing, recalling the words in Eugenie's letter. Somewhere out on the lake a loon called. Had Eugenie G. Fraser lain awake, she wondered, and heard the quavering call of the loons on Sky Lake?

Jane slid out of bed and went to stand by the window, holding the sheer curtain aside. The moon shed a path of silver across the water. The same moon, with its cold, bruised face, had shone down on the house on the rock when Eugenie had lived there 68 years ago. What terrible things had been happening in her life to make Eugenie write that letter?

Dropping the curtain, Jane got back into bed. She was shivering.

*Chapter* **3**

At dawn on Thursday, the water of the lake was so calm that when the girls went down to check it, as they did each morning before breakfast, dust lay undisturbed on its black surface. There was no hint of a breeze, not a cloud in the sky. By ten o'clock the heat had become intense. It was as if a giant lid had been set over Sky Lake, trapping the sun inside. The only way to escape the searing heat was to remain submerged in the lake, which was what Jane and, eventually, even Corrie did for the best part of the morning. Nell remained in the shade of one of the poplars, fanning herself with her newspaper, her skirt folded back above her thin knees.

After lunch Nell insisted that the girls spend an hour with absolutely no activity, and they drooped listlessly on the lawn chairs under the trees.

"Are you going to your dad's this summer?" Corrie asked, repositioning her chair out from under a hanging nest of hungry baby orioles.

"I'm not sure." Jane picked at a mosquito bite on the back of her arm. "He hasn't really invited me." The oriole parents were back, and the young were clamouring for the morsels that were being offered.

Jane was grateful that Corrie didn't persist. It was too hot to talk anyway. She had never told Corrie how her father was living the last time she'd seen him. How the great gold mining adventure had turned out.

He had come to pick Jane up during the spring break from school two years ago in his battered half-ton truck. The condition of the truck did nothing to allay Mary's fears that she had made the wrong decision in letting Jane go with him.

To Jane's dismay, Dan Covington was living in a trailer in North Bay with his sister Karen and her three children. It wasn't even a pretty trailer, like the ones in the trailer park back home, with their Florida rooms and white picket fences. This one was parked in a clearing at the end of a gravel road, its skirting of warped green plywood falling away in places, a jumble of cement blocks for a front step. Jane had had to sleep with two of her cousins, twin four-year-old girls, and even with that many bodies in the bed, she had never managed to get warm.

It had rained for the entire week. The roof of

the trailer leaked, and the family's television set was broken. Jane had found a stack of old comic books under the bed with all the dust balls, and they had proved to be her salvation. She had read those tattered, yellowed comics over and over till it was time to leave.

Her father kept telling her on the drive home, a trip taken mostly in uncomfortable silence, that he would be getting his own place soon. He'd heard there was money to be made raising chinchillas, and he would send for her again. But he never had. She had felt sorry for him and angry that he hadn't done better, and her mother was mixed up in those feelings too.

"I'm going inside," Jane announced now and, in spite of Nell's warning that heat rises and they would be better off downstairs, the girls retreated to the bedroom. Corrie lay down and picked up her book. Jane kicked her smelly runners into her side of the closet and flopped down on her bed under the ceiling fan, which stirred the warm air around the room. After a few minutes, Jane looked over to see that Corrie's book had dropped from her hands. She looked even smaller and more vulnerable in her sleep and, not for the first time, Jane felt guilty about the resentment she'd harboured when she had heard Corrie was coming to Sky Lake. They had been friends all their lives.

Even before, if that were possible. Their mothers had been bridesmaids at each other's weddings.

A full hour had passed when Jane cracked open one eye, looked at the bedside clock and realized she'd been asleep. Her face was wet with perspiration. She could tell by Corrie's movements that her friend was waking too.

"Do you think you could row a boat?" Jane asked, wiping her face with the hem of her T-shirt.

"I suppose it would be cooler out on the water, wouldn't it?" Corrie said. Her wispy bangs were plastered to her forehead. She yawned and sat up. "What did you have in mind?"

"Jess told me about a way up to the top of that big rock," Jane said. "I want to see what's left up there of the Fraser house."

Corrie reached into the closet for her hiking boots. "You aren't suggesting we actually climb that rock face, I hope."

"Not the rock itself," Jane assured her. "There's supposed to be a trail on the other side of it."

Nell was up from her own nap and sitting in front of the mirror in her bedroom, tucking loose ends of hair into her braid, when the girls stopped by to tell her they were taking the boat out. "Stay close to the shore," she advised, speaking around a mouthful of hairpins. "And be back before four-thirty. That's when I send out the search party."

"Why didn't you tell her where we were going?" Corrie held the shed door open while Jane lifted down the oars and a pair of life jackets.

Jane shrugged. "I thought she might not let us. Probably think it was too dangerous. She feels responsible for me while I'm here. You know."

"It isn't dangerous, is it?" asked Corrie.

"Not the way we're going," Jane promised. "Jess said the kids from around here go up there all the time."

While Corrie put the oar into the lock on her side of the boat, Jane pushed off from the dock and dropped onto the seat beside her. "Okay," she said. "Rowing's not hard if we do it together." The first splash of the oars disturbed a colony of water beetles which was spinning dizzy circles on the surface of the lake.

Once Jane had adjusted her stroke to that of the smaller girl to keep them going straight, they struck out along the shore in the direction of the rock. In less than twenty minutes, they entered its shadow, their boat dwarfed by the mass of granite. "It's so huge," marveled Corrie, leaning back as far as she could and looking up. At this proximity, it was impossible to see the top.

"Nell says it's more than ninety metres high," said Jane as they drifted past. "Put your oar up now, Corrie. I think I can get us in closer." She reached out, grasping for some bushes and propelling the boat forward, into a narrow cove which was almost hidden by the small trees growing out of the opposite bank. Standing up carefully, she put one foot over the side onto a slim, pebbled beach and drew the boat in close enough to tie it to a thick root at the base of the cliff.

A dirt path started upwards behind the rock and disappeared into the overhanging bushes. "That must be the trail," Jane decided. "It's kind of steep."

Unbuckling their life jackets, they tossed them back into the boat. Since this expedition had been her idea, Jane led the way, grabbing onto tree roots where she could and glancing back every now and then to see how her friend was progressing. The trail zigzagged around rocky projections, switching directions every few feet.

"Don't keep stopping," Corrie pleaded.

"I'm just checking that you're okay," Jane said, looking down over her right hip to see her.

"I'm okay, but you're kicking dirt down onto me."

After a few more minutes, Corrie gasped, "Are we nearly there? Can you see the top?"

"Yep," Jane answered, breathing hard. "Not much farther."

"Ooh, Jane! I can't look down!"

"Then don't."

One last scramble and Jane hoisted herself over

the edge on her stomach. She straightened up, brushing herself off and waiting for Corrie to do the same. The climb had brought them to the top, but well back from the edge of the rock face.

They were dirty and panting, glad of the breeze which dried the sweat on their faces. "Oh, it's heaven up here," cried Corrie, lifting her arms out from her sides and letting the wind blow through the sleeves of her shirt. She spun around slowly, arms still outstretched. "I've never been anywhere higher than this. Unless it was in an elevator. I bet there's always a wind up here."

"Me too. Look, you can see a million miles from here." Jane scanned the horizon in all directions.

Almost directly across from the rock, on the opposite side of the lake, was the stretch of sandy beach and the boat docks, the white frame building of the marina and store. Below them, five or six pleasure boats crisscrossed the lake, some of them towing water skiers. A frenzied jet boat buzzed between the boats and the island like an annoying insect.

Not thirty metres back from where Jane and Corrie stood, just as Jess had promised, was the foundation of the old house, as bare as bones on a beach.

"There it is," Corrie announced. "All that's left of your house."

An involuntary shiver ran through Jane's body. They approached the remains of the house together.

Was this then where Eugenie G. Fraser had lived? Four walls of flat stones and mortar, piled as high as Jane's waist, with two lower places where front and back entrances had been; six squat, stone pillars out front, the bases for the wooden columns supporting the verandah, which Jane remembered from the photograph. Nothing more.

They stepped down into the foundation for a closer look. There was a large fireplace in the centre, and although the chimney had long ago toppled, the fireplace, constructed of the same flat rock as the walls, was as solid as the day it had been built. It was open on opposite sides, and would have provided a hearth in two downstairs rooms of the house.

The girls circled the inside perimeter slowly, reverently, reaching out every now and then to touch the cool stones.

"Nell said the house burned down." Corrie was the first to break the silence. "Away up here though, who could've helped them put the fire out?" She stopped, clapping a hand over her mouth. "Oh, Jane! You don't suppose Eugenie and her baby died here?"

Jane looked up, suddenly chilled, expecting to

see that the sun had gone behind a cloud. But the afternoon sky was as clear as it had been all day.

"Jane, where are you going?" Corrie whirled around as Jane hurried past her and out through the front doorway. She caught up with her outside. "Are you okay? You look kind of funny."

"I'm okay," said Jane cautiously, because the uneasiness which had made her flee the house was still upon her. She lowered herself onto the rock and wrapped her arms around her knees, hugging them to her, shivering uncontrollably.

Corrie sat down beside her. "What happened?" she asked.

"I don't know. All of a sudden it got real cold in there," Jane explained. She gave her friend a sheepish smile. "I guess I'm okay now, out here in the sun."

Corrie's look was puzzled, but she said nothing. Away to the west they could see twin lakes, seeming so close you could stretch out a hand to touch them.

"You'd think," Corrie ventured, after a minute or two, "that if the house burned down, there'd be stuff lying around, wouldn't you? You know, like charred beams and stuff."

"After sixty-eight years?" Jane doubted it. "People probably used the wood to make campfires. There looks to have been lots of them up here."

"Or they could have thrown it all down into the lake," Corrie speculated. "I bet the kids coming up here did that."

"It's a long way down," Jane said, getting to her feet again and brushing off the seat of her shorts. She had recovered her composure now. "I wonder how long it would take if you dropped something over, before you heard a splash."

"You probably wouldn't hear it," decided Corrie. Instinctively, she grabbed hold of Jane's shirt. "You're not going to find out! Please don't go near the edge!" she begged.

"Don't worry, I won't," Jane affirmed. "I've heard stories of people getting too near the edge in high places. How there are these weird updrafts of wind which can suck you right over."

Standing very close to each other, they settled on admiring the view a safe body-length back. A family and their Labrador retriever had arrived by boat at the island, which they could see from their vantage point. The girls watched as each person disembarked and followed the eager dog on its exploration. "It's almost four," Corrie said finally, checking her watch. "We still have to get down from here and row back."

"Then we'd better go," agreed Jane. She sat down at the top of the trail and took one last look at the foundation of Eugenie G. Fraser's house. "I got the weirdest feeling in there," she admitted.

"Weird, like how?"

"I can't really explain it. It sounds crazy, but when you said that, about maybe Eugenie and the baby dying there, I just knew someone did." She held up her arm in front of Corrie's face. "Look, even talking about it gives me goose bumps."

"Now who's being the wuss?" Corrie teased, but she was right behind Jane on the downward trip. And Jane didn't say a word about the dirt which rained down onto her head.

After a day of such relentless heat, the thermometer only managed to drop a few degrees by evening. Nell deliberately left the washing-up until darkness fell, and the three of them lingered outside long after their cold supper had been eaten and the mosquitoes had arrived.

Nell had received the news that the girls had been to the top of the rock that afternoon with one upraised eyebrow. "I suppose you were bound to want to try it," she reasoned. "Almost everyone does. But regardless of what you think my reaction might be, I must know where you are. Understood?"

"Understood," agreed Jane.

"When were you last up there, Nell?" Corrie wondered.

"Heavens, it's been years and years. Not since Jane's mother was a little girl. You don't think these legs would make that climb now, do you?"

"The stone foundation is still there, you know," Jane said.

Nell nodded. "And I guess that was your Fraser house. There was only ever one house up there."

"We went right inside the foundation and walked all around," said Corrie. They were in the kitchen, doing the dishes together. Corrie slid another plate out of the soapy water, placing it in the rack. "I've never seen such a humongous fireplace." She looked quickly at Jane. "Something happened, though. Jane got spooked."

Nell put down the tea towel and turned to her granddaughter who was putting the clean dishes into the cupboard. "Spooked?" she repeated.

"I can't describe the feeling," Jane shrugged. "It was really weird. It was like I couldn't get out of there fast enough." She scraped at a bit of food Corrie had missed on one of the plates with her fingernail before looking up. "But one thing I do know: I *have* to find out what happened to Eugenie G. Fraser." Corrie gave her a wide-eyed stare.

The bedroom upstairs was still like an oven, and Jane dragged all the covers off the end of her bed onto the floor before dropping down onto the mattress. "I feel like Eugenie G. Fraser is begging me to find out the rest of her story," she said.

"Wow," breathed Corrie. "That's amazing. Is it

like you've been given a quest or something?"

"Kind of," Jane agreed.

"Stuff like that never happens to me. Remember when Ms. Archer asked us to pick an interesting time in our lives and write about it? I couldn't think of a single thing."

"Maybe not," Jane remembered. "But the one you made up was the best. Ms. Archer even said so."

"What she said," said Corrie, seizing her hair brush and drawing it through her hair, "was that if she'd asked us to invent an incident, mine would have been the best one."

"Oh, yeah." Jane turned on one elbow, watching her friend count the brush strokes under her breath. "You could help me, Corrie," she invited. "Help me find out what happened to Eugenie. Whether or not she escaped."

Corrie set the hair brush down. "You know how much I'd like that," she said, her small face very earnest.

Jane rolled onto her back to face the ceiling. "I'm not sure where we should start, though. I've been thinking about it a lot. The book where Eugenie's letter was found came from the store. Maybe we should start with Jess's father."

"My stars, you're up early, Jane," Nell remarked, coming into the kitchen the next morning and discovering Jane, still in her pajamas, sitting cross-legged on the bench under the telephone, pawing through the telephone directory. "It suddenly came to me, practically as soon as I opened my eyes," Jane said. "I never looked in the phone book to see if there are any people named Fraser still here on the lake."

Nell lifted one of the lids off the cookstove and peered inside. "No one that belongs to the cottagers' association," she said. "That much I do know."

Sky Lake was included in the exchange that covered the hamlets of Erindale, McIntyre and Tripp's Landing. There was only one listing for anyone named Fraser: a Simon Fraser at Tripp's Landing.

"Think it's too early to call?" Jane asked.

"I'd wait till after breakfast, at least," Nell said, putting a match to the kindling in the stove.

Agreeing to wait until no later than nine o'clock, the girls got dressed, ate breakfast, and at exactly the appointed hour, while Corrie held the phone book open, Jane punched in the number for Simon Fraser. The telephone was answered by a small child.

"Is your Mommy or Daddy there?" Jane asked.

"No," the child lisped, "just my baby sitter."

"Hello?" Another phone was picked up suddenly and a more mature voice inquired.

"Hi, my name's Jane Covington."

"You're not selling anything, are you? Because we're not interested."

"No," Jane hastened, "I'm not. I'm looking for someone, actually. I wonder if you can help me?"

"Possibly."

"I'm looking for someone with the last name of Fraser."

"Yes?"

"They'd have an older relative named Eugenie or Thomas Fraser."

"Well, I'm not sure. Could you call back after four-thirty when Mr. and Mrs. Fraser are home?"

Reluctantly, Jane agreed. "But would you know yourself if any of the Frasers ever lived at Sky Lake?"

"Not this family," the person on the other end said with finality. "I know that for sure. These Frasers came to Tripp's Landing last spring. From New Brunswick."

"Let's go back to the plan to ask Jess's father about the book where you found the letter," Corrie suggested after Jane had related the details of her conversation with the Frasers' baby sitter.

Nell had been adding items to her shopping list,

some sheets off an old calendar which lay on the counter. "Are you going for groceries today, Nell?" Jane sounded hopeful.

"We can, dear heart," said Nell, licking her pencil. "Just as soon as we straighten up around here."

\*　\*　\*

When they drove into the parking lot between the marina and the variety store, Jess Howard was pumping gasoline into two red plastic containers for a man who stood waiting at the pumps. Nell gave a tap on the car's horn, which Jess acknowledged with a nod of his head.

Setting the gas cans into the back of the customer's pickup, Jess came over to where the Lake Car had parked. "If you're still interested in that letter you found..." he began.

"We are," said Jane, opening the door.

"I don't suppose you thought to bring it. My dad would like to read it."

"It's right here," Corrie beamed, wriggling across the back seat to get out behind Jane. She smoothed the front of her tailored shorts. "Actually, we came to talk to your father."

Behind the counter at the Sky Lake Variety Store, Jackson Howard read Eugenie's letter with interest. "Intriguing, to say the least," he smiled, handing it back to Jane. "Jess was telling me about this. And after reading that, I can understand your wanting to find out what happened to Mrs. Fraser."

"Well, we're going to try, anyway," Corrie promised. "Jane and I thought, seeing as how the book came from here before it went to the sale, this was the place to start. Right, Jane?"

"In that case," Jackson Howard announced, looking pleased with himself, "Jess, show the girls what we found." Immediately, Jess disappeared into the room behind the counter.

Jackson Howard continued. "Jess has already told you how I found several boxes of those old books back there in the storeroom when I took over this place. But there was some other interesting stuff too. Old account books, handwritten receipts. So, when Jess asked me if I knew who might have run the store in 1930, I knew where we could find out."

"This used to be called a general store," Jess said, setting a heavy cardboard box onto the counter and opening the flaps. "Have a look," he invited. "Dad and I started going through this junk last night."

"What are all these things?" Jane asked, picking up a sheaf of papers held together with a rusty paper clip.

"Receipts, mostly," said Jess. "You wouldn't

believe how many people ran a tab at the store in the old days. Dad said those were hard times. Anyhow, Dad and I figured somewhere it should tell us who the owner was in 1930."

"And did it?" asked Jane.

"It did. And when I saw who it was, it nearly blew me away."

"Why?" Corrie asked. "Who was it?"

"Here. There's a receipt with his name on it." Jess passed a small square of paper over the counter.

"'D. Morris,'" Corrie read. "So who is he?"

"Here's one with his whole name on it." Jane pulled a receipt from the bundle she held in her hand. "'Desmond Morris, Prop.' Is that supposed to mean something to us?"

"To me it did," Jess admitted. "He's a guy who's living at the Seniors' Lodge in Erindale. Right now."

"Really?"

"I help out at the lodge sometimes," Jess explained. "And I know this guy. I could probably set it up so's you could meet him, even. We could talk to him, see if he remembers the Frasers."

"Could you?" Jane asked, not even trying to mask her excitement.

"Sure, if you want. He's a neat old guy. Besides, most of them over there really love to talk."

Jane turned to Corrie with a wide grin. This was much better than anything she'd hoped for.

"So if you can hang on a minute, I'll call over there right now," Jess offered. "See when's a good time to visit him." The girls waited while he went to a phone on the wall inside the door.

"Look at this stuff," said Jane happily, digging deeply into the box. "Here's a bill of sale for six pairs of rubber boots. They used to sell rubber boots here."

"A general store sold just about everything," said Nell, coming up behind them and setting her wire basket of groceries onto the counter. "I remember being able to buy yard goods here. This is where the material for the curtains in the kitchen came from."

"I have Mr. Morris," Jess was saying, his hand over the receiver. "How's four o'clock Sunday sound?"

"We'll need a ride," Jane hesitated, looking at Nell.

"I seem to be running a taxi service these days," Nell smiled. But she didn't refuse them and held out a hand while Jackson Howard counted her change into it.

Nell was winning a game of Yahtzee on Saturday night when Mary called again, sounding cheerful and happy. She was meeting her friend Joyce at a resort in the Muskokas for a few days. She talked to Jane first, then to Nell, then asked to talk to Jane again.

"I've given your grandmother the phone number at the resort, Jane. In case you need to reach me for any reason. I'll only be gone five days."

Jane could hardly believe what she was hearing. "You're going on a holiday? I thought you were having such a busy month."

"I'm telling myself I need it, to get over the trauma of turning forty." Mary laughed lightly. "So Corrie's having a good time?"

"Of course."

"And you're helping your grandmother as much as you can?" Mary persisted.

"Yes, Mother. She's got a new handyman now who does some of the bigger stuff."

"Nell didn't mention a handyman to me."

"He's just a teenager," said Jane. "His name is Jess Howard. You remember his father, Jackson Howard? Jess helps Nell when she needs him and works at the municipal centre and the seniors' lodge too, I guess."

"My goodness," Mary laughed. "Quite the go-getter."

"He said he's doing community service."

"Is that what he told you? Community service?" Jane thought Mary's voice was beginning to sound a bit shrill. "You mean, he's some kind of delinquent?"

"I don't think so." Jane fixed Nell with a quizzical stare.

"Put Mother on again, will you, Jane? I hope you're not hanging around this boy."

"I'm not hanging around him, Mother," Jane protested. "I've talked to him a couple of times, introduced him to Corrie."

"Oh, Carol will be impressed, I'm sure! He's obviously been in some kind of trouble, Jane. Put Nell on, please."

Jane handed her grandmother the receiver with a skyward roll of her eyes. She and Corrie sat on the edge of their seats, awaiting the outcome of the conversation. Nell spoke calmly for a few moments and then replaced the receiver. "There now," she said brightly. "Who wants popcorn?"

"So what is community service, anyway?" Jane demanded, getting to her feet.

"It's something a judge hands sometimes to young people who get in trouble with the law. They spend a certain number of hours working in the community and afterwards, there's no record kept of the offense. They have a clean slate, so to speak."

"Who? Jess?" asked Corrie. "What kind of trouble?"

"Did you know all along, Nell?" Jane was suspicious. "About the community service?"

"I did, dear."

"Then why didn't you tell me? At least before I opened my big mouth."

"I thought if Jess wanted people to know, he'd tell them." Nell reached into the fridge for the jar of popping corn and handed it to Corrie.

"He did tell us," Jane remembered. "But we didn't know what he meant."

"I wonder what kind of trouble it was," said Corrie again.

"I can assure you he is no delinquent," said Nell. "I trust him completely. Now Jane, the little pot for melting the butter is hanging behind the stove." As far as Nell was concerned, the subject was closed.

# Chapter 4

The village of Erindale consists of a single long street, bisected at right angles by the main highway. In summertime, the population swells to five times its usual size, and the sidewalks teem with cottagers and campers from the nearby lakes who stroll in and out of its two dozen small shops.

On Sunday, Nell arranged to meet an old friend at the local tea room while the girls and Jess were visiting with Mr. Morris. To their surprise, it was Jackson Howard who was waiting for them when the Lake Car pulled into the parking lot at the Erindale Seniors' Lodge.

"Where's Jesse?" Corrie asked as Jackson joined them to walk across the baking asphalt to the front of a sprawling, grey brick complex. Nell drove off promising to be back to pick them up in one hour.

"Jess said he'd have to catch you later," explained his father. "To be honest, he had a bit of a run-in with a customer in the store last evening

One of the cottagers who wanted to be waited on by an adult. He was probably the type of person who treats all teenagers that way, but Jesse took it personally, started sounding off to me later when I came in. I suggested that he go and cool off a while. He spent the night at Al's. He's my friend who runs the marina. Al and his wife have been good for Jesse, giving him a bit of space when he needs it.

"Anyway," he smiled, "you'll let him off the hook, won't you?"

"Sure," said Corrie amiably.

"No problem," said Jane, thinking of her own mother's reaction to the news that Jess was doing community service.

"Okay, you ladies ready?" Jackson Howard held the glass doors open while they filed inside.

"Mr. Morris isn't sick, is he?" The lodge looked to Jane a lot like a hospital, with gleaming corridors and uniformed attendants.

"No, this isn't a hospital," Jackson Howard told them. "Although there is a doctor on call and nurses in the medical wing. Jess tells me Desmond is in perfect health. He just decided five years ago that this is where he wanted to live. Sold the house he and his wife had always owned. He's a widower now, apparently."

They passed an attractive solarium, filled with

green plants and sunlight and the twitter of caged birds, and turned into another hallway where rosy carpeting muffled their footsteps.

"Jane says you knew her mother," Corrie said conversationally. "Were you, like, going together?"

"Corrie!" Jane protested.

Jackson Howard laughed. "Well, it wasn't quite like that. There were eight or nine of us, I guess. Teenagers. Some, like Jane's mother, spent summers here; others lived here like I did, year round. None of us actually paired off. Not then, anyway. We used to go places together in the evenings or on weekends. Swimming and hiking, canoeing. A couple of us had cars, so we'd go into Erindale for milkshakes and the movies. Eventually, some of the group went away to university or to find work. I went out west where the jobs were in those days.

"When Al phoned out and told me the Sky Lake store was for sale," Mr. Howard continued, "I decided I was ready for a change; my wife had passed away four years ago. So I came back here to the place I grew up and bought the shop." He took a deep breath. "I'm seeing a nice woman and trying to get my life back on track. Jesse, I'm afraid, hasn't adjusted as well to the change as he might have."

He had stopped in front of a door with a small

brass knocker. "This is it," Mr. Howard announced. "Number 37C." He lifted the knocker and tapped sharply.

If Jane and Corrie had been expecting a wizened old man, they were surprised at the elegant gentleman who answered the door. Desmond Morris was tall and slim, dressed in a blue blazer, a paisley ascot tucked into the neck of his shirt. The grey trousers were neatly pressed. He greeted them heartily, firmly shaking everyone's hands. "What? No Jesse today?" He stepped out and looked left and right down the hall to see if his young friend might be lagging behind.

"Those old codgers in B-Wing likely tired him out the other night," Desmond Morris decided good-naturedly. "Do you know the lad goes over there and plays cards with them on Friday nights? Now, cards aren't my cup of tea anyway, but I can't imagine a lad his age spending a Friday night with old folks when he doesn't have to. Pretty remarkable boy you've raised there, Mr. Howard."

"I never doubted it for a minute," said Jesse's father.

The living room where Mr. Morris led his visitors was pleasantly crowded with furniture. Family pictures in brass frames covered the walnut end tables. Among the other pieces of polished wooden furniture was a glass-fronted china cabinet, filled with ornaments and glassware, the collections of a lifetime.

"Now then," Desmond Morris began, seeing everyone seated and settling himself in a winged chair. He lifted his feet onto a small footstool upholstered in needlepoint. "Jesse tells me you children found a letter in one of my mother's books. A letter with a rather desperate message."

Jane blinked in surprise. "It was your mother's book?"

"Of course. I guess you don't know about Mother's library."

"Library?" Jackson Howard queried. "We thought you used to run the store. The accounts were kept by a Desmond Morris."

"That was my father," Mr. Morris smiled. "I think you'd find I would have to be much older than I am, had I been running the store nearly seventy years ago."

"Of course," said Jackson Howard, looking embarrassed.

"A perfectly honest mistake," Desmond Morris declared agreeably. "Never could understand why fathers and sons were given the same first name. Shows a definite lack of imagination, don't you think?

"My father, the first Desmond Morris, opened the store at Sky Lake in 1919, after the Great War, and he and Mother ran it for thirty-five years. During that time, my mother operated a small lending library there. It was really only a couple of shelves of books for the customers to borrow. There was no other library hereabouts, back then. And that would explain how the letter from the pretty lady, that's what we called her, got into one of Mother's books.

"I presume the people who bought the business in 1954 when my parents finally sold it, didn't want to be bothered with the library. They must have packed up the books and put them in the storeroom."

"Which is where I found them, years later," Jackson Howard interjected. "I gave them to the library for their used book sale."

"Then the letter we found must have been meant for your mother," concluded Jane.

"That's what it looks like," Mr. Morris agreed. "Mrs. Fraser must have put the letter into the book and returned it, either herself, or more likely from what I've heard, by way of someone else, thinking my mother would see it before putting the book back on the shelf."

"Did you know Eugenie G. Fraser?" Jane inquired.

"Not really," Desmond Morris said. "I was just a boy."

"What we want to know now," Jane pointed out, "is what happened to her."

"And her baby," Corrie added.

"That I cannot say," admitted Desmond Morris. "Not for certain, anyway. There were a lot of rumours. But I do have something to show you, something I know you will be interested in." He got up from his chair and went into the next room, returning a minute later with a framed picture. It was a painting done in watercolours, showing the rock and the Fraser house. He laid it on the glass-topped coffee table. "It hung in our home for many years," he said proudly.

Jackson Howard leaned forward to examine it, his elbows on his knees, hands dangling. "I bet there aren't too many pictures like this one around."

Desmond Morris nodded. "As you're no doubt aware, we get artists up here all the time painting pictures of the rock, but I've never seen another showing the house up there. I'll never forget the night that house burned, either. I was about ten years old, and I saw it from my bedroom window."

He walked over to stand at the picture window of the living room which overlooked a parched lawn and beyond it, the contrasting green of the woods which hid the lake. "We lived over the store in those days, and I remember being awakened that night by the sound of the fire bell. It had been a big, magnificent house, and the fire was spectacular. My mother and I were frozen to the spot. We just stood there at the windows in horror.

"The men from all around had gone over in their boats to see what they could do. But they were helpless. The dock was gone, the elevator, everything. The men came back to our place. Our store was the meeting place at Sky Lake in those days."

He turned back from the window. "You don't forget that sort of thing," he said again, shaking his head. "It was a terrible sight."

"Do you remember anything about the people who lived in the house?" Jane asked.

"Not much. There were two brothers, Americans. Thomas and Franklin Fraser. They were both inventors of some kind. They were the ones who built the house. About 1928. The lady came later. I called her the pretty lady, but I think it may have been my mother who told me that. I can't remember her, exactly."

He lowered himself into the chair again. "No one in his right mind builds a house away up there out of the way. That rock is 300 feet high! And how they built it is something else. There was no road to the property, never has been, so everything had to be taken across the lake by boat. My father told me the biggest timbers went over by barge."

"But how did they get things up to the top?" Jane asked, moving to the front of her chair, and studying the watercolor on the table again, the sheer drop between the house and the water.

"Well, these two brothers, eccentrics to say the least, were as I told you, inventors. Apparently, they designed an elevator to transport their materials, and themselves, from the dock at the base of the rock, up to the top. Quite a feat of engineering.

"We didn't see much of the Fraser brothers," Mr. Morris went on. "I don't think they were regular customers at the store. Then, that last summer, there was a lady with them. A pretty lady and a baby."

"That would be Eugenie," decided Jane.

Desmond Morris nodded. "She must have come into the store and borrowed a book from Mother's little library."

"And she must have written the letter to your mother," Jane said, excited by the feeling that some of the pieces were coming together. "Maybe the only way to get the letter out of the house was to hide it in the book. She must have thought your mother would send your father or someone over to see what was going on. Maybe bring her and the baby back."

"I would guess that was what she hoped would happen," Desmond Morris agreed. "But I'm sure Mother never got her letter. Otherwise, I know she would have done something about it. She must have put the book back on the shelf without ever finding Mrs. Fraser's letter. And there it stayed all those years. Until you found it."

"How do we know someone didn't go and help her?" Corrie suggested, looking hopefully from one face to another.

"Well, I guess we don't," Jane conceded. "Except the letter probably wouldn't have still been in the book. But that's one more reason to get to the bottom of this. Find out how it all ended."

Desmond Morris agreed. "My mother used to say those old stones up there would have quite a story to tell. If only they could talk."

"Maybe they do talk," said Jane, and the other three turned to look at her. "We were up there, Corrie and I. It was as if someone was trying to tell me something. I got goose bumps, like something terrible had happened there."

"I didn't feel it, though." Corrie's tone was wistful.

"Well, you could be right, you know." Desmond Morris made a little tent with the tips of his fingers. "The way the story went back then, something terrible did happen in that place." They all waited for him to finish. "Something the fire was meant to cover up. A murder, in fact."

Jane was the first to find her voice. "Whose murder?" she asked. "Was it Eugenie's?"

Desmond Morris let his hands drop back onto the arms of his chair in a weary gesture. "I'm afraid I don't know the whole story," he said sadly. "I never saw any of the people from the house again. My parents would have known all the details, to be sure. But in those days such things weren't discussed in front of children. You understand. Grownups protected us from unpleasantness."

"Darn it!" exclaimed Corrie.

Desmond Morris smiled. "The story, the way I heard it later, was that someone was murdered in that house before it burned down." He paused and reflected. "But then again, maybe it was only a story."

"Was it Eugenie who was murdered?" Jane insisted. "Or could she have died in the fire?"

"I think you have to be prepared to accept that as a possibility," Jackson Howard said.

No one spoke for a few moments. The only sound was the hollow ticking of the clock on the china cabinet.

"I wish someone had written all this down somewhere," said Jane morosely. "You know, like, kept a diary.

"Hey, I just thought of something!" she cried suddenly. "Don't libraries always have old newspapers? If we could find one for the day of the fire, it would all be right there for us to read."

"You're right," declared Jackson Howard. "Maybe Jess would know if the library right here has back issues of the *Erindale Echo* on microfilm. You know that the fire happened in 1930, so you could go through the papers for that year till you find the story."

"It happened late in the season," Desmond Morris said. "Early autumn perhaps. You know, in later summers, I remember, the more daring young men used to go diving in front of the rock, trying to find any remains of the Frasers' elevator. Don't know if they ever did. Some say the lake right there has no bottom."

"Really?" Corrie and Jane chorused, wide-eyed.

"Well, it's extremely deep, anyway," Jackson Howard said gently.

When the time came for the girls to meet Nell, Mr. Morris walked with them along the halls to the front door to say good-bye. He held onto Jane's hand after he'd shaken it. "I can understand your fascination with the story, my dear," he said, his voice kind. "Especially since you were the one who discovered Mrs. Fraser's plea for help."

"Thank you," said Jane, grateful that he

sympathized with her need to know the truth. "I think the very least we can do for her now is try to learn whether or not she managed to escape."

"The best of luck, then," their host said. "And do let me know what you find out."

*　*　*

The doors to the library at the municipal centre had barely opened on Monday afternoon when Jane and Corrie arrived, eager to begin their search. Jess, they immediately determined, was nowhere in sight.

"We're looking for the *Erindale Echo* for the year 1930," Jane gulped when the librarian, who had just turned the "closed" sign to its other side in the window, gave them an inquiring look. Nell headed for the comfortable chairs beside the rack which held the latest issues of the city papers.

The librarian led the girls around the corner to an area housing "Information Services" and began checking the bank of small drawers in a steel filing cabinet. "This is where we keep the microfilm," she said, but before she had found what she was looking for, she had to leave to answer the telephone. "I'll be right back," she promised.

Jane and Corrie pulled two chairs out from under a study table to await her return. "I wonder if we could find anything in the local paper about Jesse," Corrie whispered. "You know, about what it was he did to get in trouble?"

"Why don't you just come out and ask him?" Jane demanded, with sarcasm. "The way you asked his father if he was going with my mother?"

Corrie sat back, looking injured. "What was the matter with that?"

Jane winced. "It was kind of, you know, blunt."

"Mr. Howard didn't mind," Corrie pointed out defensively. "Besides, I bet you wondered about it too. If they were dating, he might even be your real father."

"Come on, Corrie! We all know my real father. Anyway," Jane spun her ball-point pen on the surface of the table in front of her, "my mother and Mr. Howard were friends when they were teenagers. She's forty years old now. I think you're taking this 'Jane's interesting life' idea a little too far."

The librarian reappeared at that point, ready to help them and preventing any further discussion. After she had opened and shut several drawers, she finally lifted out a small index card from the front of one of them. "Okay," she said, "that explains why I couldn't find anything for 1930. Here, you might as well read it for yourselves."

The card told them that the *Erindale Echo*,

which had been called the *Erindale Express* prior to 1955, had suspended publication in November, 1927. It wasn't published again until 1945. There was no local paper the year of the fire.

"The regular librarian is on holiday," her replacement explained. "She would have known right away, I'm sure."

"Another dead end," grumbled Jane, rejoining Nell. She dropped into a wicker arm chair beside her grandmother, her legs splayed out in front of her. "Just when I thought we might be getting somewhere, too." Corrie was prowling around, picking up brochures like a true tourist.

Nell refolded the newspaper she'd been reading and prepared to drop it onto the rack. "Wait a minute!" Jane exclaimed, reading the paper's masthead. "Maybe that fire was a big enough story to have made it into the city papers. I'm going to ask the librarian if they have any back issues."

Her enthusiasm was soon dampened, however. A library as small as the one at Sky Lake, the librarian explained, was lucky to have even the local paper on microfilm. "But I could try sending to one of the bigger libraries for you," the woman offered.

"Could you?" Jane asked. "That would be great." The three of them waited by the desk while she opened a library directory and began turning pages.

"Doesn't Jess Howard work here?" Corrie asked innocently.

"He's off this week." The woman paused in her search, frowning at Corrie. "Is he a friend of yours?"

"Not really," Corrie admitted, swallowing visibly. "We just met."

"The regular librarian finds things for him to do," the woman sniffed. "I'm just a volunteer. I don't have to put up with kids doing their time on my shift."

Jane stepped into the conversation. "Doing their time?" she queried.

"You know. He's a troublemaker, and he's doing community sentencing."

"I really don't think you could brand him a troublemaker," Nell said, her voice gentle. "Just for one foolish escapade."

"One brush with the law is one too many," the woman declared, her mouth drawing up like a purse. "I don't trust the kids these days. You have to keep your eye on them every minute, and I don't have time for that."

"We're kids." It was Jane's turn to be indignant. "And I don't think that's very fair. Grownups with attitudes like yours only make it harder for kids." She and the librarian glared at each other for a few speechless seconds.

Then there was nothing more for Jane to do except escape. "Come on, Corrie," she said, and turning abruptly, she headed out of the building. Nell and Corrie scurried in her wake.

"My goodness, Jane," declared Nell, catching up with her at the Lake Car and smiling widely. "I must say I'm proud of you. Taking a stand like that."

Jane was still shaking from the confrontation. "I sort of surprised myself," she admitted. "I just got so mad."

Nell swung her car door open. "Never mind. It needed to be said. Such narrow-mindedness amazes me."

"The lady was going to see if she could find some papers for us in one of the bigger libraries," Corrie protested, climbing into the back seat after Jane. "You shouldn't have lost your cool."

Jane knew that was probably true.

"Don't worry about it. Everything will work out," Nell promised. "I have an eye appointment in Peterborough on Wednesday, and I'd been wondering what you girls were going to do with yourselves while I was at the doctor's. You can spend the time at the library."

"You know, that woman's reaction wasn't much different from Mom's," Jane observed as the familiar scenery of the lake road played past the car again, in reverse. "I bet Jess gets that all the time."

"You're right," said Nell sadly. "It's doubly hard for Jesse now. He was a newcomer to begin with, trying to fit in with kids who've lived here all their lives. But now with the scrape he's had, he has to try to prove to these people here that he's a good person."

"Well, sometimes he makes it hard to be friends with him," said Jane. "I told him he has a bad attitude."

"Perhaps," Nell agreed. Jane could see just her blue eyes in the rear view mirror. "We have to try to understand that after all he's been through—his mother's death, moving here—he feels vulnerable. His prickly attitude protects him from any more wounds."

"I already figured that out," said Jane.

✻   ✻   ✻

The early morning drive to Peterborough on Wednesday was made at that pristine hour when the mist rises slowly off the fields with the approach of the sun. Everything was still, the day seeming to hold its breath.

The Lake Car crossed the Otonobee River a half hour before the library opened. "We could find a restaurant and have a cold drink," Nell suggested when Jane returned to the car after reading the notice board in front of the library.

"We'll just wait till the doors open," Jane decided. "There's a place to sit over there. You don't want to be late for your appointment." Now that they had come this far, she wasn't leaving, even for a few minutes.

"I should be back by twelve-thirty," said Nell. "Wait inside where it's cool. We'll have some lunch before heading home."

Already the air in the city was heavy with heat, and the cicadas had begun their monotonous whine in the clipped hedges around the library. When the librarian lifted the blinds and unlocked the door, the girls were grateful to enter the air conditioned atmosphere inside.

The librarian in charge of the reference room gave them the boxes of microfilm for the *Peterborough Examiner* which covered the year 1930 and made sure they knew how to thread the microfilm reader. Then the two sat down in front of the illuminated screen as Jane spun slowly through issue after issue of the paper.

At eleven-thirty, after going through several reels of microfilm, they had to admit that the mysterious fire at Sky Lake had not even been mentioned in the larger papers.

"I'm starting to see double," complained Corrie, sitting back with a groan.

Another librarian came on duty at lunchtime, and she seemed intrigued by the girls' search. "Did you take a look at the *Sizzler*?" she asked, pulling a small drawer towards her and extracting a single box of film. "It was only published for a year or two around the time you're interested in, and then it folded; but its reporters sometimes did stories from the vacation spots in the area. Why don't you have a look at it?"

And that's exactly where their search ended.

# Chapter 5

By twelve thirty-five, Jane and Corrie were waiting on the bench outside the library, almost hysterical with excitement at their discovery. Having been shown by the librarian how to make a copy of the article, they had read it aloud several times before they saw Nell nosing the Lake Car into an empty parking space. "I thought I told you to wait inside," Nell pretended to scold as the girls tumbled into the back.

"We were too excited," Jane announced, leaning out to pull the car door shut and reaching for her seat belt. "Eugenie G. Fraser got away, Nell! She didn't die in the fire."

"Why, that's wonderful!" Nell picked a break in the line of traffic and surged into it. "I figured as much when I saw the size of the grins on your faces. So you had a successful morning?"

"Finally," said Corrie. "It took some digging, too. My eyeballs are aching from all that reading."

She relaxed against the back seat and placed the palms of her hands over her eyes.

"Want me to read what we found?" Jane offered after a few moments. "The librarian called it purple prose. Said that's what the *Sizzler* specialized in."

"The *Sizzler*?" Nell eyed Jane in the mirror. "What on earth is that?"

"A vacation newspaper they used to have around here in the Thirties," explained Jane. "Here's what it says: 'Woman Tells True Story of Death House.'"

"Death house. My, my," muttered Nell.

"One night last October," Jane read in dramatic tones, "a young woman fled her stately home on the highest point on Sky Lake. Fled in utter terror. Fled on foot in the night, clutching to her bosom her young child."

"That's what it says," Corrie confirmed admiringly. "Clutching to her bosom."

Jane looked up, suddenly aware that Nell had pulled over onto the gravel shoulder of the road and stopped the car. Her grandmother turned in her seat. "Go on," she urged. "This sounds so good, I don't want to miss a word."

"Especially the way Jane really reads it," Corrie enthused. "She sounds just like an old-time radio announcer."

Jane's eyes returned to the page and she

continued. "The story she told this reporter was one so horrific as to make it almost beyond belief. Almost, but not quite. It is a tale so tragic, dear readers, that it tears at the heart strings of even this hardened reporter. Now that the court case is over, we have the full story at last.

"'He murdered my husband and then went down in the elevator and set the dock adrift,' the woman wept. 'He didn't want anyone coming to save us.'

"The accused was Franklin Fraser, the older brother of her husband, Thomas Fraser. 'I heard him coming back up, thought he was coming for me. I was frantic, trying to find a place to hide. I saw him take an axe to the supports that held the elevator, letting it fall down into the lake.'

"She gathered her wits then, and leaving her dead husband where he had fallen, snatched up their child and ran into the night, in which direction she knew not.

"She did not know the house she was fleeing was on fire until later, after she had reached the sanctuary of Mr. and Mrs. Colin Bloom's summer residence on Sky Lake.

"There she stayed until the authorities arrived and she could tell them the dreadful story. Relatives came to fetch her and, although she came back to Erindale for the hearing, she vowed she would never again return to the scene of this tragedy. A tragedy which took the lives of both Fraser brothers and very nearly cost her her own and that of the young child."

Nell was speechless.

"Isn't that something?" marveled Jane. "There's a picture too, of Eugenie and Thomas." She passed the photocopy across the back of the seat to Nell.

It was a street photographer's shot of a happy, young couple walking towards the camera, a bank of shop windows on their right. The girl had a broad, high forehead and wide, sweet smile which emphasized her full cheeks. She was wearing a flowered, summer dress and a small hat which was perched atop a mass of curly, blonde hair. Her companion, who held his hand over hers where it had slipped though his arm, as if he were afraid of losing it, was youthful and slender, a little taller than the girl. He was wearing a double-breasted suit in a light colour and a straw boater. In the sea of passersby on the city street, these two shining faces stood out.

"Now all we have to do is find this Mr. and Mrs. Colin Bloom and ask them where she went," said Jane, taking the picture back and studying it again. "Mr. and Mrs. Thomas Fraser, in happier times," the caption read. There was something disturbingly familiar about Eugenie's face.

"I keep looking at her," Jane murmured. "I can't

believe I'm actually seeing her, Eugenie G. Fraser, a real person, the one who wrote the letter. This is so cool."

Finally, Nell eased the car back onto the highway. "The Blooms are still around," she informed them, hiking herself up to the steering wheel again. "At least, old Mr. Bloom is. His wife died some years ago, but his daughter has kept the family cottage. Look! There's that chicken place up ahead. Let's stop there for some lunch."

"It's such a sad story," said Corrie. "And hearing Jane read it, gives me the shivers."

"It's quite a story, all right," Nell agreed as she negotiated four lanes of traffic. "You two are terrific detectives. Eugenie G. Fraser would be proud."

Later that afternoon, when they were on the last leg of their journey and driving once more around the lake, the girls began watching for the Bloom's place. "Where is it, exactly?" Jane asked.

"You can't miss it," Nell promised. "You know the mailbox with all the flowers painted on it? We pass it every time we go down the road. Just after we go over the little wooden bridge across the creek."

Sure enough, less than a kilometre from Nell's place, there was the green mailbox covered in painted flowers. "That means," Jane realized, "that Eugenie must have gone right past My Blue Heaven that night. Why wouldn't she have stopped there?"

The Lake Car bounced into Nell's driveway and lurched to a standstill. "She must have missed it," said Nell, collecting her bags off the front seat. "She probably headed north off the rock, and must have worked her way east, finally coming back down towards the lake again, after she was past us. At any rate, it would have been quite a hike for her, especially in the dark and carrying a baby. And when I think of the horror she was running from. Can you imagine watching while that man cut off any means of rescue or escape?" Shaking her head, Nell turned towards the back door.

\* \* \*

"Are you looking at that picture again?" Corrie teased, buttoning her blouse after they had had a swim and were changing out of their bathing suits. "You'll wear it out, you know."

Jane had taped the picture above the light switch inside the bedroom door. "I feel that if I look at her hard enough, I'll find out more about her," she admitted, her eyes fairly burrowing into the paper.

Corrie examined the picture over Jane's shoulder. "She wouldn't look like that today, you know," she said. "This has to have been taken at least seventy years ago. Anyway, I have something else for you to look at." Corrie opened the top drawer on her side of the dresser. "But I don't want you to jump down my throat." She handed Jane a folded flyer. "Remember those brochures I picked up at the library the other day? There was one about community sentencing. It tells all about the program Jess is working under."

Frowning, Jane opened the paper Corrie put into her hand. "Have you been charged with a minor criminal offense?" it read. "Are you under 18? Are you sorry about what you did?"

\*　\*　\*

There was a "Sold" sign on the Blooms' cottage at the end of the lane. Rose Bloom, a short, stocky woman with blue-tinted hair and several strings of beads on her ample chest, greeted the girls at the back door and led them through sun-filled rooms which smelled of the morning's toast and coffee. "Dad's feeling a little sad this summer," she confided. "This will probably be his last trip up here. I couldn't keep up this place and the house in the city. So we've had to let the cottage go. He's going to miss it."

The girls could see old Mr. Bloom sitting on the deck under a striped umbrella, gazing out at the lake. "It's beautiful here," breathed Corrie. It was a far cry from Nell's rustic My Blue Heaven.

Below a varnished deck which shone like glass, the terraced lawn was lush and well-trimmed. The poplar and birch trees with their white bark stood out against the deep green of the grass and provided dappled shade. Purple phlox spilled down the sides of the stone steps to a carpeted dock and the lake.

Rose hesitated before opening the sliding door. "It's funny you should have phoned yesterday," she said, "asking about Mrs. Fraser and the time she came here. Why, just the other day when I was packing up some things, I came across a card she must have written to my mother. A thank-you note." She slid the door open and they stepped out onto the deck.

"Now, I've told Dad what it was you wanted him to remember. So he's expecting you." She came around the old man's chair, wrapping her arm around his thin shoulders. "Dad, these are the girls who wanted to see you. Remember, dear? They were wondering about the time the lady from the house on the big rock came here with her baby. Remember that? The night the big house up there burned down?" She had indicated two chairs on the other side of the glass-topped table, and Jane and Corrie drew them in closer, smiling encouragement at the elderly gentleman.

The pale blue eyes which gazed in their direction were watery, far away.

"Remember, Dad?" Rose prodded, taking his hands. "We were talking about it last night. Her name was Eugenie and she had her baby with her."

"I remember," the old man's voice quavered. "Of course, I remember."

"It was a murder-suicide, you know," Rose said to the girls, wrinkling her nose. "Two brothers."

"The baby cried all the time," the old man offered. "Dora and I put them up here. They were soaked through. Must've been raining. Yes, that's right."

"Go on, Dad."

"They came to our door. We could see the fire, the whole sky to the west was lit up. Up on the rock, it was. She had come from there, on foot, running through the brush with the baby. She could hardly talk. We didn't know who she was, even." He paused then and looked out at the lake where the sunlight was dancing. He seemed to have forgotten where he left off.

"Dad told me she stayed two or three days with us," Rose said. "Then some people came up from the States to fetch her. Isn't that right, Dad?" She smiled encouragingly. "From the States?"

"That's right," the old man said, and his head kept nodding long after he'd finished speaking.

"Some days he's better than others," Rose said, when a few moments had passed in silence. "Now you girls just sit still, and I'll go get that note Mrs. Fraser wrote to Mother. And some apple juice too. Dad always likes his juice this time of morning. You'll join us, won't you?"

"Can you believe this place?" Corrie whispered, after their hostess had gone back inside. "That grass makes me want to go and roll on it."

Jane nodded, but she felt an ache in her heart for the old gentleman in the beige cardigan, who wouldn't be able to enjoy this view another summer. For the first time she understood the importance of having someone like herself, or Jess Howard even, for Nell to turn to; what peace of mind it must give to Mary. If help weren't at hand, would Nell eventually have to stay home? Put My Blue Heaven up for sale?

"Here we are!" Rose bustled out again. She carried a tray with a pitcher of juice and four glasses. Setting it down, she handed Jane a small, cream-coloured card, with a bouquet of mauve violets decorating the front. "That's the note I found in Mother's things."

When Jane opened it and saw the familiar handwriting, she thought she would burst into tears. How much time had elapsed, she wondered, between the time Eugenie G. Fraser had penned the first letter and this one? The note was undated.

Bedford, Massachusetts.

My dear, dear friend:

I cannot thank you enough for everything you and your husband did for us. Now that that is all behind me, my baby and I must start a new life. I will never be back to Sky Lake, and because this means I will probably never see you again, this makes me sad. But I know you will understand.

Give little Rose a hug for me, won't you?

My deepest thanks,
Eugenie G. Fraser

P.S. If she could talk, Mim would send her love.

"Mim?" Jane looked up. "Who's Mim?"

"Her baby," Rose explained. "Mimosa."

"A baby girl," said Mr. Bloom, unexpectedly. "Like our Rosie. Had the most peculiar name."

"You know, that's funny," observed Jane, passing the card to Corrie. "I met a woman on the bus coming up here the other day. Her name was Mim."

"I wouldn't think there'd be too many Mims in this world," remarked Rose, getting to her feet. "Come along now. I'll walk up the lane with you to see if the mail lady's come."

"It could be the same person," said Jane, hardly able to contain her excitement until they had said good-bye to Rose Bloom, and she and Corrie were turned in a homeward direction. "The woman on the bus had inherited property here. Someplace. That's why she was coming here. I don't know where it was. But it could be her! She could be Eugenie's daughter! Oh, Cor, I've got to find out! She was staying at the Bide-a-Wee cabins. We've got to call them and get her address. Then we can write and ask her if Eugenie and Thomas were her parents!"

"That would be so amazing," Corrie agreed. "But wait a minute. If your lady on the bus inherited the property from her mother, and her mother was Eugenie, then that means Eugenie is dead."

"I know," Jane agreed reluctantly. "I guess, even though I knew it was impossible, I'd hoped we would find her looking just like she did in the picture. That she'd be the pretty lady Mr. Morris told us about."

They were crossing the little bridge over the creek when Corrie suddenly stopped. "Eugenie must have come down right about here," she realized.

"Here where the creek comes down to the lake."

A few steps more and they reached the other side. "I think you're right," said Jane, looking around. "She came to the creek, and rather than try to cross it, she decided to follow it down. That would have brought her here to the road."

"Maybe she stood on this very spot," Corrie suggested, her eyes getting very round. "Imagine!"

Jane nodded. She knew what Corrie meant. It was like being a part of history, of everything that had happened before in this place. "But remember, she was running for her life. So she wouldn't have stood anywhere for very long."

"She'd have had to stop to catch her breath," Corrie pointed out. "Maybe change arms, with the baby."

"Maybe," agreed Jane. "And she saw lights down there, through the trees, the Blooms' place."

"Maybe she was stumbling and falling even, hanging onto the baby, thinking Franklin was behind her."

Jane stepped up onto the embankment above the road. "I'll bet she came through right here," she said. She began to walk up the slope, through the tall grass, between the stands of sumac with their candle-like flowers, still a light shade of green this time of year.

"Where are you going?" Corrie demanded, clambering up the bank after her. "I thought you wanted to call the Bide-a-Wee."

Jane hesitated, wiping the sweat off her upper lip with the side of her forefinger. "Yeah, you're right. But sometime, I'd really like to try retracing Eugenie's footsteps that night."

"That would be so cool."

The sight of something up ahead caught their attention. One of those igloo-shaped, pop-up tents made of blue nylon sat on the bank, further upstream. "Funny place to camp, isn't it?" Corrie commented, looking around nervously.

"Not really. I remember coming up here myself to fish with Nell when I was little," said Jane. "There used to be nice little brook trout in this stream."

"Yech!" said Corrie, turning on her heel.

They made their way back through the long grass again, and rounding a clump of cedars, almost collided with someone coming up the embankment. Head down, intent on his ascent, Jess Howard didn't see the girls until he was almost upon them. A backpack was slung over one shoulder and a fishing pole stuck out of the top of it.

"What are you doing here?" Jess demanded, stopping in his tracks.

"We were just out walking," Corrie stammered, sounding too apologetic to Jane.

"Well, well," said Jane. "If it isn't the long lost

Jess Howard. You sure know how to make yourself scarce. We thought we'd see you at the library, to say nothing of the seniors' lodge. And aren't you the one who's just a little far from home?"

"I'm camping." Jess eased the pack off his shoulder onto one of the rocks at their feet, scowling at the girls. "Didn't you see my tent?"

"We saw it," Jane shrugged. "Come on, Corrie." Then she stopped; she couldn't resist asking, "How's the work on that attitude going?"

"Okay, okay," Jess winced. "It's a free country. I didn't mean to chase you off."

"You didn't," Jane assured him loftily. "We have to get back anyway and make an important phone call." She gave Corrie a little nudge to get her started again, but Corrie seized that moment to sink down onto a rock with an exaggerated sigh.

"Man, am I bushed!" she exclaimed. "I just can't go a step further."

# Chapter 6

Jane drew a long stem of grass toward her and bit off the sweet, white end. "So," she said in the awkward pause which followed, "How come you're camping, instead of working?"

"I have a week off," Jess explained, playing with the straps on his backpack. "They told me to take a holiday. Because of the heat. I don't work at the library when the regular librarian's away anyway. I'm just doing some fishing and thinking." He eyed them both narrowly. "Mostly thinking."

"So, what's there to think about?" Corrie put up a hand to shade her eyes.

"Oh, how I messed up my life, and stuff. I guess you know about the mess I'm in. Right?"

The girls nodded. "Some of it," Jane admitted, sitting down to share Corrie's sun-warmed rock. "That you're doing community service."

"Okay. Then you must know about me borrowing my dad's truck and having the accident?"

When they shook their heads he went on. "Geez, I thought everyone knew about it."

"Do you really think the whole world has nothing to do except think about you?" Jane asked.

"I didn't think you were old enough to drive," said Corrie.

"I'm not, officially," Jess admitted. "But I can. Out west we ran a garage. Dad always let me move the vehicles around the lot. Drive them into the shop, park them outside when they're ready for the customers. It was cool." He had taken a seat on a rock opposite the one the girls had chosen. Removing his baseball cap, he hit it against his knee and returned it to his head, wearing it backwards this time.

"Then we came here. I hated it. Hated the kids, the school. Heck, we came in November! The school year had already started. I had to walk into practically the middle of grade 10."

The girls said nothing. Jane decided he must need to talk about this. He seemed to be on a roll.

"So this one day, I was kind of showing off for a couple of the guys. I took Dad's truck out. I didn't think there'd be any ice. Like, it was April! Everything was melting. But in this one place I guess the water had run across the road all day, and then at night it froze.

"Anyway, there was this little jog in the road. I

guess I hit the brakes. I mean, I hardly touched them! But we went into a spin. It was unreal. I could see the edge of the road getting closer, but there was nothing I could do. We went into the ditch and broke through this guy's fence."

"We?" asked Jane "There was someone else with you?"

"A guy from school. Cougar, they call him. He was able to get his door open, so he took off. Just like that. 'I'm outta here, man!' he said, and he was gone."

"Nice friend." Jane pulled up another piece of grass.

"Yeah, well. All of a sudden I see the lights come on in the house, and this guy in a housecoat comes running out, telling me to stay where I am, that his wife's calling the police."

"I bet you wished you could wake up, then," said Corrie fervently. "That you'd find out it was all only a dream."

"You got that right," Jess snorted. "Anyway, I got charged with property damage under a thousand dollars. 'Course, by the time I got to school Monday, everyone knew about it. That I had to go to court. Here I'd been trying to impress these guys, and now they treated me like I was anything but cool. So I just thought, what do I need them for? They're all just a bunch of losers."

"Really?" Jane gave him an incredulous look.

Jess shrugged. "I had plenty of friends back in Vancouver. And just as soon as I'm eighteen, I'm heading back out there. Ditching this dump."

"Yeah, right!" said Jane.

"You don't believe me? Just watch me!"

"What about your dad?" Corrie cut in quickly. "He seems really nice. How did he react?"

"Oh, the usual. You know. Said I must have left my brains back in Vancouver." Jess laughed lightly. "No, actually he was pretty cool about it. He went to court with me and signed the application for the community sentencing. I got forty hours of community service to do.

"The lady with Social Services took me around to meet the people at the municipal centre and the seniors' place. They're okay. I do mostly outside work. When the weather's no good, I put in a bit of time at the library. I'm nearly done now. I'll have enough hours in at the end of July. But you know how it is. I feel like people are, like, watching me? Waiting for me to mess up again."

"They probably aren't, you know," Jane told him.

"Aren't what?"

"Waiting for you to mess up. Everyone just gets on with his own life. No one sits around waiting to say, 'Ah hah, I told you so'."

Jess looked at her for what seemed to Jane a long time. As if he were seeing her for the first time. Jane felt her cheeks growing warm, and she had to look away. Finally, Jess gave another shrug. "You could be right. But who cares? Vancouver was the best. Dad's family came from around here, and that's maybe why I feel people are watching me. You know? Like I have to measure up? Like, when I heard your mother knew my father, I knew right away you'd hate me."

"Why?"

"Because I wouldn't be anything like you expected."

"I didn't expect anything!" Jane protested. He really was exasperating. "I didn't even know my mother knew your father. Anyway, what does it matter?"

"Okay, so maybe not everyone knows I got into trouble," Jess allowed. "Young offenders' names aren't released to the media, but people find out anyway. Erindale's a small place."

"I think the best part is once you finish your hours you won't have any record," Corrie spoke up, and when Jess looked puzzled, Jane explained, "Corrie's been reading up on it."

"No kidding," said Jess, with some surprise. "How come?"

Corrie flushed and looked down at the back of her

hands, spread on her suntanned knees. "I saw this brochure in the library, and since you'd said that's what you were doing, I picked up one to read."

"Yeah?" Jess was clearly impressed. "You know about the alternative measures deal?"

"A little," Corrie admitted with a shy smile.

The look Jess gave Corrie made Jane wish that she too had read the brochure. Corrie always knew the right thing to do or say when it came to boys, Jane thought. She had considered Corrie's motive for wanting to know more about the community sentencing program as just plain nosiness. Jess, on the other hand, seemed to see it as someone wanting to understand his experience.

"I don't have to show up in court till I'm finished my hours of service," said Jess.

"And you start all over again with a clean record," Jane reminded him. "That's pretty good."

"It's cool," Jess agreed. "Like, I get a second chance."

"So someone must have thought you deserved it," Jane pointed out.

"True."

"So, that should prove to you that not everyone is on your case. Right?"

Jess bent over the milkweed pod he was dissecting. "You know, it's kind of funny," he said, looking up with a wry smile. "I told my dad I wanted to go camping, try living off the land, you know? And this morning he leaves me two bags of groceries down there in the hiding place we said we'd use if we needed to get in touch. I guess he didn't want me to starve."

"Parents!" Jane said fondly. "You know, if you run out of food you could always come down to Nell's. She never lets anyone go hungry."

Jess nodded. "Your grandmother's pretty cool. Like, she knew I couldn't get a job this summer, having to do my hours and everything? So she told me she could use me as her handyman whenever I could spare the time."

"Nell's special, all right," Jane concurred, flicking bits of grass off her lap and getting to her feet. "Okay. Now that we know the whole world isn't talking about Jess Howard, would you like to hear our news? Do you want to know what we found out about Eugenie G. Fraser and that letter she wrote? The one you and I found in the book?"

Jess shouldered the pack again. "My dad told me about Mr. Morris having the painting of the house on the rock, that she lived there."

"That's right, with her husband and his older brother," Jane said. "The men had built the house up there a couple of years before she came here."

"What about the brother she was afraid of?" Jess remembered.

"Well, turns out she had reason to be scared," said Jane. "The one brother murdered the other. Eugenie's husband Thomas was murdered by Franklin Fraser. Then he must have set the house on fire. But Eugenie got away, and Franklin must have killed himself. She escaped with her baby whose name was Mim, and she ran all the way to the Blooms' cottage that night." Jane stepped up onto the rock to point out to Jess the cottage they had visited earlier, but its roof was hidden by the trees.

"We found all that out in the newspaper," said Corrie, no longer trying to be modest. "We've been to the library in Peterborough and everything."

"But the best part is," Jane concluded, "that I think I might have met Eugenie's baby daughter."

Jesse gave her a look of disbelief. "Wait a minute," he protested.

"No, really. Well, of course she's not a baby now. I met this woman on the bus when I came up here a couple of weeks ago. She was coming to look at a piece of property she had inherited on Sky Lake. Her name was Mim."

"The same name as Eugenie Fraser's baby," Corrie finished, triumphantly.

"That's a bit of a stretch," said Jess.

"Maybe not. We're going to call the place where

she stayed when we get back and get her home address from them."

"Cool," said Jess. "Look, are you two hungry? Want to share some spaghetti with me? I haven't caught any fish yet, but Dad left me two big cans of spaghetti. If you want to."

"It's not that we don't want to," said Jane, "but this phone call is pretty important."

"I guess." Jess nodded. "You'll let me know how it all turns out, right? I'll likely be going home tomorrow."

"Listen, I've got an idea. Why don't you come back to Nell's with us?" Jane invited, surprising even herself. "We can make our phone call, and I know Nell would be happy to have you to stay for supper."

"But I've got all this food," Jess grimaced. "I either eat it or have to lug it all back home."

"Well, at least come while we make the call," Corrie urged. "Then you'll know how it turns out."

"Okay, I could do that," agreed Jess. "Hang on a sec."

Corrie and Jane waited while he sprinted up the hill to his tent and set his backpack inside. "Surprise, surprise," murmured Jane, when Jess reappeared and started down towards them again.

"Well, I'm not the least bit surprised," Corrie declared stoutly. "He likes you. Can't you tell?"

When the three turned into the driveway at My Blue Heaven a few minutes later, they could see Nell outside on the deck chair, her book open in her lap. From the angle of her head it was apparent she had fallen asleep.

"Let's not disturb her," Jane advised, opening the back door carefully and letting the others slip inside. "We'll make our phone call first. Corrie, do you want to get us some cans of pop? Grab a chair, guys."

The number of the Bide-a-Wee was printed on a folder which listed the businesses on Sky Lake and which Nell kept posted by the telephone. "My grandmother and I dropped a lady off there on July third," Jane began, when someone answered the phone at the tourist cabins. "Her name was Mimosa Granger."

There was silence at the other end and then the sound of pages being turned. "Yes. That's right."

"We were hoping to get in touch with her again," Jane continued, "and wondered if you had her home address."

"I'm afraid I can't give you that information."

"Oh," said Jane. "My grandmother is Nell Van Tassell. On the north shore here? My Blue Heaven?"

"Right," acknowledged the Bide-a-Wee. "And your grandmother should know we can't give out information such as the home addresses of our customers."

"Ms. Granger was visiting from the States," Jane went on hurriedly, before he could hang up. "She had inherited property here on Sky Lake."

"Right," agreed the man again. "I can tell you she was with us only one night. Sorry, I have another call coming in." And Jane was left with the sound of the dial tone.

"They didn't tell you?" Jess asked. From Jane's expression it should have been obvious.

"Couldn't. He's not allowed to give out that information." Jane took the can of root beer Corrie handed her and pulled back the tab. "Thanks," she said, taking a swallow. "If we could just find out if the property Mim inherited was on top of the rock, that would be the connection we need. Then we'd know for sure she was Eugenie's daughter. I can't believe I'm saying this, but I wish Mom was here. She knows all about properties and stuff."

"Could we somehow find out who pays the taxes on the property on the rock?" Corrie suggested from her place at the table. "That would be the person who owns it, wouldn't it?"

"Wow, Corrie," exclaimed Jane. "Great idea!"

Jess emptied his drink and got to his feet. "Dad pays our taxes right there at the municipal office. They have tons of records, and there's a big map on the wall of all the lots on the lake. That should be the place to look."

The back door opened and Nell entered the kitchen, looking surprised to discover them there. "Ah, girls, you're back. And Jesse. How nice! I've just come in to make some iced tea. Will you join me, or maybe you want to take a swim."

"We've all had a cold drink, thanks," said Jane. "And I for one am definitely going to hit the water. But first, we're dying to tell you our news. Here," she grabbed the back of a chair and pulled it out from under the table. "Sit here, Nell. You absolutely are not going to believe this coincidence."

Nell listened with interest to the details of the visit to the Blooms, and with incredulity to Jane's deduction that the woman who had come to Sky Lake on the bus with her was Eugenie's daughter.

"Mimosa is an unusual name," Nell admitted. "But I'm not so sure, dear. And I'm not at all surprised the Bide-a-Wee didn't give you her address."

"Well, I figure we could find out if this Mim person owns the property on the rock, if we ask over at the municipal centre," said Jess.

"You may be right," Nell nodded. She looked around at three expectant faces. "Next, I suppose you'll be asking me to take you over there."

Jane seized her suddenly from behind. "Oh,

Nell, would you please?"

With a wry smile, Nell stood and pushed her chair back in. "I told your father the other day I seemed to be running a taxi service this summer, Jesse. Now you see what I meant. You coming with us, by the way?"

"I'd like to," Jess said, sounding undecided. "But I'm camping up the road a bit, by the creek."

"Come for the ride then," Nell suggested. "We'll bring you back."

Jess hesitated. "Would there be time for me to pack up all of my stuff and go back with you? Save Dad a trip tomorrow night? If that's okay."

"Perfectly okay," Nell assured him. "The girls are going to have a swim anyway. So why don't we meet you at the road in, say, an hour?"

✳  ✳  ✳

"Hi there, Jesse." A young woman in a red mini dress and sandals got up from her computer behind the counter in the municipal office and approached the teens. "How's it going?"

"Good thanks, Debbie," Jess replied.

Debbie's brow furrowed. "Were we expecting you today, Jesse? No one left me any orders."

"I'm still on holiday," Jess explained. "These are friends of mine, and we need some information."

"Okay," said Debbie, agreeably. "Shoot. What do you want to know?"

"Is it possible to find out who owns a certain piece of property on the lake?" asked Jess.

"Sure. Do you know the location of the property?"

Jess looked questioningly at Jane.

"Or who the neighbours are?" Debbie added.

"There aren't any neighbours, really." Jane said. "The property is at the top of the big rock."

Debbie turned to the large map of the township on the wall behind her. "Right here," she said, putting a manicured nail on a spot on the far side of the lake. "Okay, I'll just take a look at the assessment map." She went into the other office for a minute, then returned to do a search on her computer.

"Here we are. The owner of that property is Mrs. Eugenie Fraser," she announced.

"Eugenie!" Jane gasped. "You mean, she's alive?"

Corrie's look was puzzled. "I thought you only inherited stuff when someone died."

"Oh, sorry," the girl at the computer frowned. "I should have said 'the estate of Mrs. Eugenie Fraser'."

"Is there an address?" Jane ventured to ask.

"Of course, dear. We do have to have that to send out the tax bills." The young woman wrinkled her nose. "But it's illegal to give out a person's address. Sorry."

"I never knew so many things were illegal," Jane grumbled as the three started back to where Nell sat in the car, with all the doors open.

"That's the way it goes, I guess," said Jess philosophically.

"If we had an address for Eugenie we could write to her family, at least," muttered Corrie.

Nell got out of the car as they approached. "So?"

"Eugenie's dead," said Jane, kicking at the gravel. "The property belongs to her estate."

"Oh. Her estate. Well, you can't be too surprised, dear."

"Not really, I guess," Jane admitted.

Jess was collecting his backpack and camping gear from the trunk of the car. He hoisted the bag containing his tent onto his shoulder. "Thanks for the lift, Ms. Van Tassell," he said. And to Jane, "Sorry my idea didn't work out." He looked as if he meant it. They watched him saunter off in the direction of his father's store.

As the Lake Car headed for home, its occupants were all wrapped up in their own thoughts. "Isn't it kind of weird that Eugenie held onto the property all those years?" Corrie asked, after a few minutes. "I mean, she said in her letter to the Blooms that she'd never come back here."

"Maybe it was just too painful for her ever to deal with," Nell suggested.

"Traumatic," Corrie decided. "That's the word I was looking for."

"Stop here, Nell!" Jane shrieked suddenly.

"What on earth!" Nell slowed the Lake Car to a stop on the edge of the road, just past the Bide-a-Wee cabins.

"Corrie and I will get out here and walk on around."

"Why would you want to do that?" Nell demanded, throwing her arm up onto the back of the seat.

"We're going back to talk to the owner of the cabins," said Jane. "Maybe if we ask him face-to-face, he'll tell us Mim's address."

"I seriously doubt that," Nell said. "He said no once."

"Well, it won't hurt to try." Jane had already slid out of her seat.

"It's a good two miles back to our place, Jane," Nell reminded her, concerned. "Are you sure you want to walk in this heat?"

"We'll take our time. Come on, Corrie. Promise we'll be back by four-thirty, Nell." Slamming the door of the car, Jane stepped back into the dust-covered weeds at the side of the road, giving Nell a peremptory wave.

Corrie watched in open-mouthed disbelief as the Lake Car drove off without them. "What do you think we're going to do now?" she demanded, her hands on her hips.

"We're going to walk back to the Bide-a-Wee and somehow get a look at the guest register."

"You've got to be kidding! Besides, their records are probably all on computer."

Jane hesitated for an instant. "Well, maybe not. The place didn't look very modern to me. Now listen, if someone comes in while we're looking at the register, we have to have a reason for being there. Maybe we could say we're collecting brochures on all the area attractions."

"I wish you'd just leave me out of this," Corrie groaned, tramping behind her.

"Look, Corrie. How are you ever going to have a more interesting life if you never take any chances? Come on. We're in this together. Remember?"

"I remember. But this is getting too scary. Maybe even illegal."

"Please, Corrie," Jane said, walking backwards to plead with her. "All I'm asking is that you help me think of an excuse for coming here. You won't even have to go inside."

"Oh, all right." Corrie picked up the pace. After a moment or two, "Maybe we could say we're working on a project."

"In the middle of summer?"

"Well, it's the best I could come up with on such short notice."

They had reached their destination. A circular driveway, enclosing a large bed of red and white geraniums, fronted the main office of the Bide-a-Wee cabins. Behind it, tucked into the fringes of the woods, were eight or ten small cabins, like dollhouses, with window boxes and gingerbread trim.

"All we have to do is get into the office so we can check the book," Jane determined.

"What if there's someone in there?" asked Corrie as they started around the driveway to the office.

"We'll just have to get them out."

"How?"

"I don't know. Maybe create a disturbance?"

"Not! Someone might call the police."

"I was only kidding," Jane told her.

"How can you?" Corrie moaned. "At a time like this!"

"I've got an idea." Jane suddenly brightened. "I could say I was here with my parents a while back and lost something. That I've come back to see if they found it."

A car moved down the driveway past them and turned in the direction of Erindale. A maid was pushing a cart with a load of linen and cleaning supplies along the path of red bricks which connected the cabins. She didn't look up. The girls walked towards the door of the office, Jane craning to see inside as they passed the window. In the shadow of the shrubbery, they stopped.

"Did you see anything?" Corrie whispered.

"I didn't see a computer, anyway," Jane replied. "There's a counter with a rack of postcards and stuff, and a door to another room behind. Okay. Wait here." She gave Corrie a small shove and her friend, trembling, stumbled into the bushes to the left of the entrance. "I'm going in to have a look."

"Be careful!"

Jane opened the door and stepped quickly inside. There in front of her, just as she'd hoped, was a large open book. All at once, a man in a short-sleeved shirt, stood up from where he had been arranging items under the glass counter, startling her. "Hi," he smiled. "May I help you?"

"I hope so," Jane gulped. "I was here a couple of weeks ago with my parents, and I think I left my sunglasses in the cabin we were in."

"Which cabin did you have?" the man asked. Then, without waiting for her to answer his question, he came around the counter and went to the window. "I didn't see your car come in," he said.

"Oh, my parents dropped me off," Jane improvised. "They've gone down to look at the boat launch." She gave what she hoped was an embarrassed laugh. "They're kind of peeved with me, since these were the second pair of glasses I've lost this summer. They made me come back and ask you. Do you have a lost and found?"

"We do. Sunglasses? We get lots of them left behind. Do you want to come and take a look? I keep a box in my office with odds and ends."

"Well, actually, they were my sister's glasses. Just a sec." Jane stuck her head outside. "Corrie? Come in here, will you? They do have a lost and found. Since the glasses were really yours, maybe you should try to identify them."

She yanked the reluctant Corrie inside. "It makes more sense that you go and take a look," she explained. "Since they were your glasses and I was just borrowing them."

The man frowned. "You girls are sisters?"

"She's adopted," said Jane. She pushed Corrie towards the gap in the counter. The man opened the door to the inner office while Jane, smiling hugely, remained on the other side of the counter, the registration book within easy reach.

"Well, here's what we picked up already this summer," the man said, reaching for a box on the shelf to the left of the door in the other room. Corrie started rifling though its contents, and Jane spun the book around to face her.

\* \* \*

"I didn't know what you wanted me to do!" Corrie wailed when they were finally out of earshot of the bewildered proprietor of the Bide-a-Wee.

"You were amazing!" cried Jane, stopping her sideways dance up the road to go back and throw her arms around her friend. "Dropping that box was a stroke of genius. I didn't know how far back I was going to have to look to find Mim's name. But we've got it! We've got Mim's address in Massachusetts. Oh, Corrie, you were magnificent!"

Corrie looked down at the owl-eyed, mauve frames in her hands, unable to hide her pleasure at the nerve she had mustered. "I picked the ugliest pair of sunglasses he had," she said. "I figured no one else would bother to come looking for these. We actually stole them, you know."

"If it will make you feel any better, you can take them back when this is all over," said Jane. "I'm already composing a letter to Mim in my head. We can write it tonight."

"A letter?" Corrie's expression turned to grief. "Do we have time for a letter? I've got to go home next week. What day is this? Thursday? Oh, Jane, I've only got till Tuesday!"

# *Chapter* 7

"W e're home!" Jane called, and Nell, who ha
been floating motionless on her back out i
the lake, righted herself long enough to raise a
arm in acknowledgment. Her terry beach coa
hung on the pipe at the end of the dock, its sleeve
playing with the breeze.

"How much money have you got?" Jane aske
when Corrie had retrieved her wallet from upstair
and dumped its contents onto the kitchen table.

"Twelve dollars and forty-seven cents," Corri
said, still counting.

"That's way more than we need," Jane sai
assuredly. "Even to call the States. I just want t
have the money when the phone bill comes in." Sh
pulled the pitcher of iced tea out of the fridge an
poured a glass for each of them. There was
macaroni salad covered with plastic wrap on the to
shelf, waiting for their supper. "Massachusetts isn'
so far away. It's just one of the New England States.

Corrie moved the forty-seven cents through the circles of condensation on the table while the operator found the number for Mimosa Granger at her address in Bedford, Massachusetts. Jane waited, her heart pounding. It had all come down to this. This one phone call. If Mimosa Granger said she was the daughter of Eugenie G. and Thomas Fraser, all the loose ends would come together.

"Oh, no!" Jane groaned, clamping her hand over the mouth piece. "I've got a machine! She's not home!"

"That's okay." Corrie came to stand beside her. "Just leave a message. She can call us back."

"This is going to sound pretty weird," Jane began, talking quickly into the telephone, "but I'm wondering if you might be Eugenie Fraser's daughter? Oh, wait a minute. My name is Jane Covington and we met already. Remember when you came to Sky Lake and you and I sat together on the bus? Well, that was me."

She turned to face the wall in an effort to collect her thoughts, wishing she'd written down everything she wanted to say. "A lot's happened since I got here. I found out about a woman named Eugenie G. Fraser who lived in a house on top of the big rock. The house isn't there anymore, but Mrs. Fraser's estate still owns the property. Her daughter, who was only a baby when the house burned down, well, her name was Mimosa, like yours. There wouldn't be any other reason to connect you, except that you were here to see your property, and you both lived in Bedford, Massachusetts.

"I've got a picture of Eugenie and her husband Thomas from an old newspaper, and I could send it to you if you liked. What started me on all this was I found a letter Eugenie wrote 68 years ago, and I've been trying to find out what happened to her ever since. The house she lived in burned down. Did I say that already?

"The best thing my friend and I found out was that Eugenie and the baby had escaped the fire." She swung around then to face Corrie, relieved that it was almost over. "Anyway, if any of this makes any sense, you can call us at my grandmother's cottage." She repeated the number and hung up, feeling the prickle of nerves in her palms and armpits.

Nell came inside a few moments later, swinging her rubber bathing cap and patting at the braided crown of hair. "By the look on your faces, I'd say that you got what you were looking for at the Bide-a-Wee."

When the girls told her about how they'd tricked the proprietor of the tourist cabins into leaving the register unattended, Nell feigned horror. "Oh, Jane. You didn't!" She was having trouble keeping the corners of her mouth from turning up into a smile. "What a nerve! But how do you account for the fact that your lady's name is Granger? Eugenie's child's name was Fraser."

"Simple," Jane explained, "she's probably married."

Nell shook her head. "I'm pretty sure she told me she was single, dear. You may not have the right person."

"I just have a feeling about it," Jane insisted. "It just feels right to me, that the Mimosa I met on the bus is Eugenie's daughter. And Eugenie's picture, Nell. Don't forget that. All along I felt I recognized her. Mim had the same fluffy hair. You know how her cheeks are kind of chubby? That nice smile? Anyway," she said resignedly, "all we can do now is wait." She shot Corrie a glance, knowing that wasn't going to be easy, with everything in place and Corrie's days at Sky Lake now numbered. "Corrie called home to see if she could skip the family reunion and stay here till we heard from Mim."

"But that didn't work," Corrie sighed. "Dad has promised his sister from Scotland that we'll all be there. They are still coming for me on Tuesday. No matter what."

Although the girls haunted the kitchen all

evening, no call came from Mimosa Granger that night. "I'm sure she'll phone tomorrow." Jane was still confident when they went up to bed later that evening.

"Even just to tell us it was the wrong number," Corrie agreed dismally, trailing behind Jane on the stairs. "Wouldn't that be a waste of time?"

✳   ✳   ✳

All day Friday, so that at least one of them was within earshot of the phone at all times, they did things in shifts. Nell kept trying to shoo them out from underfoot, but had to admit at supper time that the kitchen had never been so well dusted and perfectly straightened.

"Whoever it was who got your message must have thought we were crazy," Corrie grumbled as the day came to an end and the sun slid down once more behind the rock in the west.

"Try to be patient," Jane pleaded. "Maybe she's out of town, or something."

"It's pretty hard to be patient, Jane," Corrie reminded her. "When I have to go home in less than four days."

Saturday dawned hot and still, and although the sky was a brilliant blue at breakfast time, the forecasters were predicting an ominous change in the weather. "Thunderstorms, possibly heavy at times," a female voice announced as the girls came into the kitchen through the back door. Nell shushed them with a finger to her lips, a frown creasing her forehead.

"Be advised that there could be high winds and hail accompanying the storm, which is tracking eastwards. Expect it to hit cottage country later this afternoon."

"Boy," exclaimed Corrie, "it sounds like it could be pretty bad." She sprinkled cereal flakes into a bowl on the table. "Good thing we took Jess home when we did."

"Oh, you can't always believe the weather forecasters," said Jane, folding her hands in front of her on the table. She was going to wait for Nell's oatmeal.

"Nonetheless, I think I'll have you put another rope on the boat, Jane, after you've eaten." Nell was stirring the porridge. "We wouldn't want to lose the old girl."

The wind was whipping up little whirlwinds of sand at the back door, and the boat was rocking rhythmically against the dock when they went down to ensure it was tied securely. "This is the most fun time to go for a swim," Jane said, looking out at the lake, which was beginning to seethe. "Nell's in the house, in case the phone rings, so let's get our bathing suits on, and go and jump in the waves."

By the time they were changed and down to the lake again, the water was crashing over the end of the dock and flinging spray far up onto the rocky shore.

"It's too rough for me," Corrie determined at once.

"Oh, no. It's wonderful!" cried Jane. She didn't wait for Corrie to change her mind, but plunged in. "The water gods are angry today!" she yelled, coming up for air, flinging wet hair out of her eyes and discovering that Corrie had retreated halfway up the bank, where she stood hugging her arms and shivering.

A wave hit Jane fully in the back of the head and she leapt up into the middle of it. "This is the most fun!" she shrieked, turning to watch for the next wave rolling towards its crest, promising to be even bigger than the last.

By the time she'd finally exhausted her strength and climbed up on shore, Corrie had gone inside. Without warning, the wind picked up the lawn chairs from the front of the cottage and spilled them, end over end, down towards the lake. Jane dropped her towel and raced to rescue them. From inside, Corrie and Nell had seen what was happening and hurried out to help. For the next few minutes they scrambled around, collecting loose objects which needed to be anchored or stored inside, even unhooking the old hammock and throwing it into the shed.

Then they waited, hearing the first rumblings of thunder in the distance.

Late in the afternoon, just before the storm hit, the sky took on a peculiar, greenish tinge. To Jane, standing with the others in the sun porch, the landscape looked like Oz. The trees, the dock, the opposite shore stood out in sharp relief, backlit with the eerie light.

From the porch, they watched the storm coming towards them, first the wind with renewed strength, followed quickly by the rain, peppering the dry ground and spraying through the screens.

"Quick, get inside!" Nell hurried them ahead of her and shut the French doors to the main house. "Jane, go upstairs and see that your window is shut."

The wind was driving the rain into the bedroom, the curtains already half soaked. It took every ounce of Jane's strength to get the window closed. Within seconds of the storm's hitting, the power went out.

"That's all right," said Nell, reassuringly. "It's still daylight, but we can light the lamps and be ready in case it stays out for long. Pretend we're early settlers." She lifted two oil lamps with glass chimneys off the hutch in the living room and carried them into the kitchen. Holding a match to the cloth wick, she turned it up until she was satisfied with the circle of light it shed. Then she replaced the chimney. "There. Isn't that lovely? It's the way this place used to be lighted."

With the doors and windows secure and the fire hissing in the cookstove, it was warm and cosy, and they could almost pretend the rain wasn't battering the front of the cottage. After supper, they played Crazy Eights in the yellow glow of the oil lamps, ignoring the shadows which filled the corners of the room.

At the end of the game, Nell announced that she was turning in early, taking one of the lamps with her. "You're not really going to bed, are you?" Corrie demanded, unbelieving. "How can you, in a storm like this?"

"We've had storms before," Nell smiled. Her shadow lengthened and then disappeared.

"Now we've only got one light," said Corrie in a small voice.

"Oh, we've got tons of old candles in the buffet drawer," Jane remembered. "We can have all the light we want." Taking a handful of matches from the box in the cupboard by the stove, she melted a little pool of wax in the bottom of half-a-dozen saucers and pressed the stub of a candle into each of them. Then the girls sat down again on the couch, their feet up on the coffee table, listening to the wind and the rain. The room was filled with the scent of sulfur and hot wax.

Shadows danced on the walls, retreated and leapt upwards again. "It's like a séance," Corrie murmured, her eyes sparkling. "All these candles. Whose spirit would you call up, Jane, if you could? Eugenie's?"

"First, I would," Jane said, considering, her arms enfolding an embroidered pillow against her chest. "Then, maybe Franklin's."

"You'd call up a murderer?" Corrie was aghast. "Why?"

"So's I could ask him why he did it."

The candles sputtered and flared, the wax spilling over to create knobby trails down to the saucers.

"You know what I always do in a thunder storm?" Corrie asked, changing the subject. "I always count the seconds between the lightning and the thunder. That way you know how close it is. I get really scared when they're very close together."

"Like now!" cried Jane, slapping the cushion over her face as lightning cracked and the cottage reverberated with thunder, almost simultaneously. There was a lull for a moment. The candlelight fluttered.

"Listen," Corrie whispered, clamping an urgent hand on Jane's arm. "There's something banging. Can't you hear it?"

"Is it the door to the shed?" Jane strained to hear.

"No, we locked that," Corrie said. "Remember?"

"It sounds like it's on this side," Jane determined. "It has to be the door to the crawl space."

"You've got a crawl space?" Corrie shrieked.

"It's where the water pump and all that sort of junk is. There's a little door on this side of the cottage. You can't stand up in it, but it's okay for storage."

"I saw a movie once where this psycho murderer was hiding out in someone's crawl space! I wish you hadn't told me we had one here."

Jane looked from the flickering light of the candles on the table to the deepening dark around the room. "What time do you think it is?" she yawned.

"Where's your watch?"

"Upstairs. I left it there when I went swimming."

"It must be ten," Corrie decided. "I remember the clock bonged nine times while we were still playing cards."

The door to the crawl space continued to bang. Jane got to her feet. "Well, I've got to do something about that door, Corrie. Otherwise, it could get torn off, and with this much rain, it could fill with water."

"Can't you just wait a little while?" Corrie begged. "You're going to get soaked."

Suddenly, a furious rapping sounded at the back door. The girls leapt together in terror on the couch. "What was that?"

"Someone's at the door!"

"It can't be!"

Jane crept to the doorway between the living room and the kitchen. Sure enough, a face was visible in the glass of the back door, rain distorting its features. Whoever it was, was rapping and turning the knob frantically. "They're trying to get in!"

"Didn't you lock it?" Corrie hissed, her back pressed against the living room wall, her face mirroring her fear.

"It is locked," Jane whispered. "But I'm not sure if the front one is."

"Ooh, Jane!" Corrie was close to tears. "What are we going to do? You have to wake Nell!"

"Oh, please." It was a woman's voice. "It's me!"

"A witch!" Corrie screamed and immediately dived for the couch. But Jane instantly realized who the stranger was and, crossing the kitchen, she turned the knob on the dead bolt with one hand, opening the door with the other. Mim

Granger, dripping wet, burst inside.

"Oh, my goodness! I was afraid you weren't here at all. I knocked and I knocked."

At almost the same time, Nell, in her flannel nightgown, long braid down the middle of her back, entered the room from the opposite side. "Miss Granger," she said evenly, as if she were used to receiving travellers at her door in the midst of every storm. "How very nice to see you again."

Jane stepped aside to allow the visitor to collapse onto the nearest chair. "We didn't think anyone would be out tonight," she admitted, wondering how they could have gotten so panicked. Cautiously, Corrie reappeared from around the corner, and Jane introduced her to the woman who had shared her trip to Sky Lake three weeks earlier.

"How did you get here?" Jane asked while Mim untied the plastic rainhat and let her hair loose. A puddle was forming around her on the floor.

"I drove." She sounded sheepish. "Can you imagine? What a night! I rented a car at the airport and came here to Sky Lake directly. Then I was sure I'd lost my way. I kept driving, figuring I might eventually end up back where I began. But then the road just ended. There was this big yellow checkerboard, and I couldn't go any further.

"All around the lake there was total darkness.

The lightning at least helped to show me that there were cottages behind all the trees I could see in my headlights."

"Where were you going?" Corrie asked, finding her voice at last.

"I was coming here! I got Jane's message and I took the first flight. I tried to call you from the store, but there was something wrong with the line. The young man there said he hadn't seen you today, but figured you were all home. His father wanted me to wait, but I knew they had no accommodation. I thought maybe I'd take a chance on finding the Bide-a-Wee again, but I must have driven right past it. Everything was so black!"

She sagged against the back of the chair with a relieved smile, her arms dropping to her sides, the rain running off her coat onto the floor. Nell had been bustling around, filling the kettle at the sink. "With the electricity off, our pump isn't working, but there's enough water in the tank to make you a hot drink. Jane, hang up Miss Granger's coat for her, dear. I'm sure it's been a long time since she's eaten."

"It's Mim, please," said Mim wearily, lifting her feet out of her sodden shoes and letting Corrie take them to dry behind the stove. "I have a small bag of things in the car."

"Well, you're not going out to get it tonight,"

said Nell. "There's a spare bedroom upstairs, and I can find you some dry night clothes, I'm sure."

"I really don't want to intrude," their visitor insisted in a weak voice. "But I just had to come. I haven't stopped to catch my breath since I listened to your message on my answering machine on Thursday, Jane."

"Then, you are Eugenie G. Fraser's daughter?"

Mim nodded. "I am. And ever since my mother, Eugenie, died last March, I've been trying to find all the pieces to the puzzle. There was always something missing. I had some of the pieces, and when I heard what you had to say, I realized that you might have the rest of them.

"When I came up here a few weeks ago and saw that the property I'd inherited was so inaccessible, I went back home again, thinking I'd just put it up for sale. I had no idea that my parents had ever lived on that land. You said their house had burned, Jane. That Mother and I escaped. But my father? What happened to him, I wonder?"

Nell hurried to the table with a stack of buttered toast, which she'd made over the stove. "Eat," she directed. "Then we'll talk."

The food smelled wonderful and Jane had to restrain herself from reaching for the first slice. She shook her head at Corrie's quizzical expression. It was obvious that Mim didn't know the fate of the two Fraser brothers.

Warmed by the wood fire, sitting in the circle of light which the oil lamps afforded, Mim told them her part of the story. "I was raised by my mother and her parents, the Grangers, in Bedford, Massachusetts. I grew up thinking my father had been killed in the war. The only picture I ever saw of him was one Mother kept on her dresser all the time. A very handsome man in an army uniform." She wrapped both hands around her mug of tea.

"When I was old enough to wonder which war he might have been killed in, I remember Mother saying that he hadn't been killed in a war, exactly. But she insisted he'd died serving his country. Later, when I pressed her, Mother used to say the event was too painful to discuss, and being an obedient child, I let it alone. My grandparents were gone by then, so there was no one else I could ask." Mim took a sip of the hot tea.

"Then, earlier this year, after her death, when I was putting some of poor Mother's things away, I took the picture of my father for my own room. But as I handled it, the little leather frame came apart and I discovered the words 'Acme Leather' stamped on the back of his picture. I didn't have a photograph of my father after all. It was a stock photo which had been sold along with the frame."

No one spoke for a few moments. It seemed to

Jane as if everyone was feeling Mim's disappointment.

"The rest of the story isn't a happy one, dear," said Nell, sitting down herself then and putting a gentle hand on Mim's forearm. "Maybe you should get some rest. We can talk about this in the morning."

"But first, I'd really like to see the picture you told me about." Mim leaned towards Jane. "The one of my mother and father."

"The girls may show you that," Nell agreed, sitting back in her chair.

"Oh, Jane. Let me?" begged Corrie, forgetting the dark at the top of the stairs.

"I'll go with you and carry the candle," said Jane.

They felt their way up the stairs in the candlelight. "She doesn't know," Corrie whispered in disbelief.

"I know," affirmed Jane. "It's going to be an awful shock when she finds out her father was murdered by his brother."

"Let's just show her this picture for now," Corrie suggested, holding the candle while Jane carefully peeled the tape back from the wall. "They look so happy."

"What about the letter her mother wrote? Her cry for help," Jane wondered. "It is the next step.

It might prepare her for the worst." She opened the drawer of the dresser and slipped two pieces of paper into the pouch on the front of her sweatshirt. "I'll take these downstairs anyway and see how it goes."

Corrie set the picture of Eugenie and Thomas Fraser in front of their guest with a flourish. For a moment Mim said nothing, only stared. Then finally, "Oh, my dear. Will you look at how young they are. So that is my father."

Nell reached for the box of tissues and set it on the table, pulling one out for herself.

"My handbag," Mim remembered, looking up with bright eyes. "Here, let me show you something." She withdrew a brown file folder and shook a stack of letters, still in their envelopes, onto the table. She fanned them out in front of her. "I found these in an old suitcase among Mother's things," Mim explained. "It was filled with clippings and all these old letters. I've spent hours reading them and trying to make sense of it. Her life was a secret, and consequently, so was much of mine.

"I learned Mother had been in Boston when she was about twenty, and somehow had met the older Fraser brother, Franklin. These are all letters from him, the later ones postmarked Sky Lake, Ontario, Canada. She had cut things out of the newspaper too, and one clipping that she saved was about a convention of American inventors. Franklin's name was mentioned, along with that of a younger brother, Thomas.

"In one of Franklin's letters he tells her that Thomas is coming to Boston, something about patents for a couple of their inventions. This must have been when she met the younger brother for the first time. There's a marriage certificate too, so I gather Thomas did not go back to Sky Lake for some time. Also my birth certificate. I was born in March of 1930. Franklin's letters stop after that."

For the next few minutes, they all scanned the various bits of correspondence Mim had displayed for them. "Corrie and I talked to a man whose parents ran the store here on the lake at the time you lived here," Jane volunteered. "Desmond Morris was only a little boy at the time, but he remembers the summer there was a pretty lady and a baby at the house on the rock."

Mim nodded. "My father must have decided to return to Sky Lake and brought Mother and me to meet my uncle. I can't help wondering how Franklin must have felt. It is obvious from his letters that he was obsessed with Eugenie."

They were getting to dangerous territory now, Jane realized. To her surprise, it was Nell who took over the story, choosing her words with obvious care.

"Your mother felt unsafe, dear, and wrote to the only person who'd shown her any kindness while she was here. That was the letter which Jane found this summer."

"I have it here," Jane volunteered.

"I'd like to see it," said Mim.

"Jane?" Nell was nodding.

Jane pulled the letter out and placed it in front of Mim. "This is what got me interested," she admitted. "This letter, and then visiting the place where the house had been. And hearing Mr. Morris talk about the terrible fire."

"But you're leaving something out," Mim insisted, looking puzzled. "The fire. Nothing about anyone escaping except Mother and me. What about my father and his brother? Could they even still be alive?"

Nell got to her feet. "Perhaps we really should get some rest," she said nervously. "We can continue this in the light of a brand new day."

"Oh please," Mim begged, reaching a restraining hand towards Nell. "You don't really think I can sleep knowing only part of the story, do you?" Her voice was very calm. "It is obvious from this letter that Mother thought she was in some kind of danger."

"After Mr. Morris told us about the fire," Jane began, "he said the gossip in those days was that it had been set to cover up a murder."

"Go on," urged Mim. "It wasn't merely gossip, was it?"

"Here." Jane glanced quickly at Nell and then handed Mim the second piece of paper. "Corrie and I found this in the library in Peterborough. It's a photocopy of an article that ran in the newspaper the year of the fire."

Mim read it. Then took up the letter and read it again. She helped herself to another slice of toast and dipped the tip of her knife into the saucer of strawberry jam, spreading it slowly. All the time her eyes moved from one piece of paper to the other where they lay in front of her. "Can you imagine the tension in that house? Imagine the tortured Franklin trying to put Eugenie out of his mind?"

"It was a big house," Jane reminded her. "Maybe they all managed to stay out of each other's way."

"Something in him must have snapped," Mim decided. "And now," she waved the piece from the newspaper, "this is how it ended. My father, poor Thomas; poor, foolish Thomas who might have kept them all safe by staying away, was murdered."

"But you and your mother escaped," Corrie pointed out.

"No wonder she never told me the truth," Mim continued, as if Corrie had not spoken. "And I adopted some strange cardboard man in a World War I army uniform as my father."

When at last there seemed to be nothing more to add to the story, the girls took one of the lamps upstairs to prepare for bed. The rain had become a gentle patter on the roof above them.

"I think Eugenie G. Fraser must have been awfully naïve," Jane declared, sitting on her bed and peeling off her socks. "She must have known from his letters that Franklin was in love with her. But still she came with his brother and their baby to stay in the same house with him."

"What about Thomas?" Corrie asked, carefully folding the clothes she had been wearing. "He must have known what his brother was like. Why would he risk bringing Eugenie here? To show her off?"

Jane nodded slowly. "More and more I see Franklin as a tragic figure."

"Not me." Corrie stated. "I see Eugenie Granger Fraser that way. She had to build a life from the ashes. And she tried."

"But she made some wrong choices." Jane tossed the socks into the corner and pulled her pajamas out from under the pillow. "She should have told Mim the truth. It's worse finding out years later."

They heard the two women come upstairs and went across the hall to say good night. Nell was turning down the sheets in the spare room. The girls hovered in the doorway. "Will you be all right? Will you be able to sleep?" they asked.

"I hope we don't all have nightmares after this," observed Corrie.

Mim turned with a smile. It was Eugenie's face. "When I think of the dream I had the night before I came up here the first time, I understand now what it meant."

Nell had produced a flannel nightgown from the dresser drawer and, shaking the folds out of it, laid it on the bed for her guest.

"The only part of the dream which still puzzles me," Mim continued, "is the part where I'm riding in a helicopter."

Nell paused, her hand on the doorknob. "I'm not sure we can arrange that for you, my dear," she said.

"I didn't say my theory about dreams works every time," Mim conceded.

# Chapter 8

Jane and Corrie slept late the next morning. The bedroom was already filled with brilliant sunlight when Jane awoke. Sliding out of bed, she padded to the window.

Except for the mass of leaves and twigs strewn across the lawn, the world outside looked freshly washed. Below the window, Mim was stretched out on the long deck chair, wearing one of Nell's straw hats, her legs covered with a beach towel. A gentle breeze ruffled the waters of Sky Lake and rattled the leaves of the poplars.

Downstairs, Nell was pouring coffee into two mugs when Jane entered the kitchen. "It's a day to break your heart," Nell remarked, setting the coffee on a tray to take outside.

"That's a weird thing to say," said Jane, plugging in the toaster.

"What I meant was, the sky is so blue and the air so clean it makes one's heart ache with joy to be alive." Nell paused, tray in hand at the door, waiting for Jane to open it for her. "Oh, by the way, dear, Jess called. Wanted to know if our visitor had arrived."

Jane dropped two pieces of bread into the toaster, pressed the lever down and hurried to get the door. "Jess called? Did he want to talk to me? I mean, to us?"

"No, dear. He just said his father was worried about Miss Granger after she left there during the storm. I've asked Mim to stay here just as long as she wants." Nell edged past her. "She's exhausted, poor dear, in need of a good rest. She actually seemed to be relieved that we weren't hurrying her off. I think we're going to be good friends."

Even before the breakfast dishes were cleared away, the morning brought another visitor to My Blue Heaven. The sound of tires crunching on the gravel in the driveway was followed by the slamming of a car door. "Halloo?" someone hailed, and the back door opened to reveal, to everyone's surprise, Jane's mother.

"Mary!" Nell cried, dropping the dish cloth she was using to wipe the crumbs up from table. "Come in!" She wrapped her daughter in a warm hug, drawing her inside. "Come in and meet our house guest." Mim was sitting in the rocking chair, watching the kitchen clean-up crew at work.

"What a surprise!" Nell exclaimed happily. "Can you stay? Let me have a good look at you." Finally, releasing Mary's flushed face from between her two upheld hands, she stepped back to take a breath herself.

Jane found herself hovering worriedly, waiting for an explanation for her mother's unexpected appearance. Mary Covington had never been a person who did things spontaneously. Was there bad news? Maybe it was something about Dad. "Is anything wrong, Mom?" She followed her into the living room where Mary removed her jacket.

"Not a thing, dear," Mary smiled, laying the jacket over the back of a couch. She put an arm around Jane's shoulders and guided her back to the kitchen. "I had a lovely three-day holiday, but Joyce got called home suddenly on business. So, rather than stay on at the lodge by myself, I decided to take the last couple of days of my vacation to drive over to Sky Lake and see my family."

"And we're delighted that you did," Nell said firmly. "You haven't had breakfast, dear, so sit down. What will you have?"

"Not a thing, Mother, thanks."

"Bacon and eggs? Waffles, maybe?"

"Really, Mother, I mean it." Mary tugged at the waistband of her slacks. "I think I gained ten pounds. I absolutely gorged myself over there. So much wonderful food. Well, maybe just a piece of toast, so I can try your homemade jam."

Mary's late breakfast turned into an early lunch for everyone else, and they all lingered at the table and shared the story behind Mim Granger's presence at My Blue Heaven. The clippings and letters were laid out for Mary to read.

"And the copy of the picture, Jane," Nell urged. "Where's the picture of Mim's parents? You'll see a definite family resemblance, Mary, between Mim and her lovely mother." Nell extricated the photocopy from the other pieces on the table and held it at arm's length, squinting, as she read the caption aloud for her daughter.

"Mother, what are you doing?" Mary demanded, as Nell adjusted the distance between the page and her eyes. "Can't you see properly? You must need new glasses."

"I'm having new ones made, dear," Nell assured her gently. "They called Friday, as a matter of fact, to say they were ready. We'll go to fetch them one day this week."

"And not a minute too soon, I'd say," Mary remarked. "Why don't we go tomorrow, while I'm here to take you?"

"There's no hurry, dear." Nell got up to dry the dishes which sat in the draining rack. "Later in the week will be soon enough."

"I don't really want you taking the Lake Car all that distance, Mother. That decrepit old monster shouldn't be allowed on the road."

"We went to Peterborough in it last week," Corrie volunteered.

"In that case, I'm glad I didn't know about it," Mary said. "Look, we'll all go. What do you say? Make a day of it."

There was little enthusiasm for that suggestion. "Tomorrow is Corrie's last full day here, Mom," Jane pointed out. "She doesn't want to spend it cooped up in a car." And all that Mim requested was that she be allowed to stay put. "If no one objects to me lounging around, that is."

"Well, I guess it's just you and me, Mother," Mary said. "It'll be like old times."

"I do have house guests." Nell hesitated. "You're sure you don't mind keeping an eye on these two teenagers, Mim?"

"We'll keep an eye on each other," Mim promised. "It will be lovely."

"I talked to your mother last night, Corrie." Mary turned to her. "Told her I was coming here today. We decided I can save them a trip to fetch you on Tuesday." She smiled then at Jane. "And if Nell decides she can spare you, Jane, you can come home with us too."

"It's not a case of being able to spare Jane," Nell

stated. "Mim is here now, so I won't lack for company. If Jane wants to go home, she needn't feel she's deserting me."

Already? The day after tomorrow? Jane hadn't planned on going home so soon. What was there to do back there anyway? "I'll think about it," she said. And after a moment or two, "There's one thing I have wanted to do all summer, though, and that's call Dad. If he wants me to come see him, I guess I should go home and get ready."

"Fair enough," Mary agreed. "Would you like to do it now? I have my card with me, so your grandmother won't be charged for the call."

"Come on then, everyone," said Nell, herding the others together and steering them toward the door. "Let's the rest of us go outside. I need to give my poor flowers some attention after the storm. And if anyone feels like having a bit of exercise, they'll find a leaf rake in the shed."

So it was decided for her. They left Jane alone in the kitchen. While she gathered her thoughts, Jane set the empty dish drainer under the sink, folded Nell's tea towel and hung it behind the stove. Finally, she picked up the phone.

She knew the North Bay number by heart. "Hi," she said when a man answered. "Is this Dan Covington?"

"It is."

"This is Jane, Dad."

"No kidding? Jane. Where are you?" His voice sounded the same, husky from the cigarettes, and warm like she remembered. She pictured him the last time she'd seen him, still slim and dark, wearing one of those shirts he preferred, with the snaps instead of buttons; the western boots. His curly hair was getting thin enough on top that she could see his scalp. She had teased him about going bald, before realizing he was sensitive about it.

"I'm at Sky Lake," Jane said. "Nell's place. Remember?"

"Of course, I remember. Had some pretty good times there myself. Always was a neat place. So, how are you?"

"I'm fine. Nell's fine. Having a great summer. Lots of interesting stuff happening. I go into grade nine in September, Dad."

"High school. My, my."

"What about you, Dad? How are you?"

"I'm fine too, Janey. Working hard. I have a little lawn maintenance company going. In the winter I'll be ploughing snow—people's driveways. Have a couple of contracts to do, the odd factory. I'm not rich, but doing okay. Hope to have a place of my own soon.

"Talk about lucky breaks, though. I ran into an

old buddy of mine up here a couple of weeks back, and he told me there's money to be made by investing in this new wonder product. It's something that makes your car's engine run cleaner and smoother. Burn less fuel? So, I'm trying to set some cash aside..."

"Dad," Jane interrupted.

"Yes, honey?"

"Don't believe everything you hear. Okay?"

"Ho, ho! Do you sound like your mother!"

The porch door creaked and someone crossed the living room. Mary put her head around the doorway to the kitchen, her eyebrows upraised in a question. Jane's nod indicated that everything was all right.

"How's your mother doing, by the way?" Dan asked then.

"She's fine. Busy. Do you want to talk to her? She's right here."

"No. That's okay. Well, I'm real glad you called, Jane. Call me again sometime."

"Okay, Dad." Jane turned to face the wall, wrapping herself in the telephone cord, her voice low. "Dad, I was thinking," she murmured. "Maybe we could get together sometime?"

"Sure thing," heartily now. "I'll call you the next time I'm down your way. Oh, hold on a sec, I've got another call."

Jane made a face at her mother and waited.

"Okay." Dan was back. "It's one of my customers, so I've got to go. Got to take care of business, you know. Ha, ha."

"I know," Jane said. "Okay. So, bye Dad." He had already hung up. She put the receiver down, her hands shaking.

Mary was beside her quickly, putting an arm around her shoulders, pulling her close. "Are you okay, sweetie?"

"I'm okay, Mom." Jane swallowed and smiled. Because she was okay. "He sounded really good."

"And?"

"He said he'd call me the next time he's down our way. But he won't, will he?"

"Maybe someday he will," Mary said into Jane's hair. "No, I'm sure he will. When he grows up."

"You know what, Mom?" Jane said, as they went out the front door together to join the others. "They must've got the TV fixed. It was blaring in the background."

Mary stooped to pluck a mauve aster from the brick planter below the steps where Nell was deadheading flowers. "Your flowers look wonderful this summer, Mother. I wish I had the patience for gardening. I see you've had all the old planters repaired."

"You didn't notice that I had the steps painted

too, and the shed," said Nell, sitting back on her heels.

"Actually, I did notice," Mary admitted. "The old place is looking pretty sharp these days. Should I be complimenting your new handyman? Jack Howard's boy?"

"You should, indeed," declared Nell.

"Okay, I admit I jumped to conclusions about him. I hope I get to meet him while I'm here."

"Shove over," Jane muttered agreeably, climbing into the hammock where Corrie lay, giggling.

\* \* \*

The fresh air and more of Nell's home cooking seemed to revive their American visitor, and by the time they saw Nell and Mary off to Peterborough after lunch the next day, Mim's face bloomed the way it had when Jane first met her, and the music had returned to her voice.

In the early afternoon, Jane and Mim were basking in the warmth of the sun porch, Corrie having disappeared upstairs. "When we were coming up here on the bus," Jane confided to the older woman, "I had a feeling there was something mysterious about you."

Mim shook her head. "It was my life which was the mystery, dear. I was just an ordinary, recently retired lady, in need of a holiday." She looked up from the clippings in her lap. She had not been without them for more than a minute or two since her arrival. "I didn't even know my proper last name, before I opened that suitcase of Mother's and saw my birth certificate. And I still didn't know if my father was alive or dead. Until last night.

"Mother's will left everything to me, and discovering her cache of documents finally gave me the answer to the question about how I came to be the owner of a piece of property in Ontario, Canada." She took a deep, satisfied breath. "Now I can look at this picture you found and see my father for the first time."

"There might be other relatives of the Fraser brothers somewhere," Jane suggested. "Maybe even some better pictures of your father."

"That's possible," Mim agreed, smiling radiantly. "Now I should be able to find them."

Jane left Mim relaxing and went in search of Corrie. She found her folding clothes upstairs in the bedroom, removing things from hangers, sorting her toiletries.

"What's the hurry?" Jane asked, dropping onto the side of her bed.

"Oh, you know me," Corrie said. "I like to be all organized. I'll pack my suitcases tonight, just leave out what I'll need for the trip home." She looked up then and her face crumpled with disappointment. "Oh, Jane. Promise you'll call me if anything exciting happens."

"Like what?" Jane asked. "I mean, what else can happen? We found out how Eugenie G. Fraser's story ended. And as a bonus, we found her daughter."

Corrie sighed and bent to fold the arms of a cotton sweater. "You know what I mean," she insisted. "You just seem to have all the fun. And I go home to a boring old family reunion and a bratty brother. Who has probably been ransacking my stuff for the past two weeks. When are you coming home, anyway?"

"I'm not sure. At first, I was only staying till the end of the month. But now," Jane laid back on the bed, spreading her arms, feeling very lucky indeed, "who knows?"

Corrie yanked some long hairs out of her brush and dropped them into the waste basket. "Oh well, I have to get my stuff ready for back to school."

"That shouldn't take a whole month."

"Mom has a shopping trip planned to Toronto for the week after next. She says I need a new wardrobe for high school. Some different outfits."

"Not too different, I hope," said Jane.

"Oh, there you are." Mim stood in the doorway.

"You know, I've been thinking. Didn't you say you'd been to see what was left of my father's home here on the lake?" She stepped into the room.

"Corrie and I both went up there." Jane moved over so that Mim could join her on the side of the bed. "I thought you might have had someone take you over by boat, when you were here the first time."

"I didn't bother, dear. It was so remote. I planned at the time to go home and make arrangements from there to put it on the market."

"People go up to the top all the time," Jane said. "Corrie and I could row you over there this afternoon, if you liked. If you wanted to see the rock up close."

"I was hoping you'd say that," Mim confessed, beaming. "Do you think it would be all right with your grandmother?"

"Nell lets us do anything," declared Corrie happily, the packing already forgotten.

Jane got to her feet. "Well, almost anything. But we're all looking after each other today, anyway. So why not? Better bring jackets. It'll be breezy out on the water."

Mim sat in the bow of the boat, leaning forward eagerly, a hand on the gunwale on either side, looking as if she were leading an expedition. They followed the shoreline to the rock, and all conversation died as they drew alongside the massive wall of granite. "Now, that is truly something," said Mim, finally. The rowers put their oars up and let the boat drift. "Truly amazing. You really get no idea of its height, do you, till you are right up against it." She leaned backwards, holding her hat against her head. "Imagine a house up there! Your grandmother gave me a picture of it from her album."

Jane rested her elbows on her knees. "You're the one who should have it," she said.

Beside her, Corrie was peering over the side of the boat, searching the depths of the lake. "It's kind of creepy, what Mr. Morris said. About there being no bottom to the lake right here."

"I think that's only an expression," said Jane. "It's deep. But of course there has to be a bottom. Do you want to see where the trail is, Mim, to the top? Along here in the cove." They manoeuvered the boat into the narrow slip, and Jane held it against the shore by way of the bushes.

"I would have no trouble climbing up there," Mim declared, surprising them. "What do you say we try it?"

Jane frowned. "Are you sure?"

"I'm sure. I'm in pretty good shape." Mim swung a pair of sinewy, suntanned legs around to show them. "I ride my bicycle every day at home. I'd really like to try it."

Jane hesitated. "I don't know."

"It's very steep," Corrie cautioned.

"I can see that it is," Mim said evenly. "There looks to be plenty of handholds, though."

"Okay," agreed Jane, with a little reluctance. "Hang on, then. I'll get out and tie us up."

They unbuckled their life jackets, and Mim put Nell's hat in the bottom of the boat. Jane led the way upwards, with Corrie in the rear. Mim proved to be as well-conditioned as she'd promised and reached the summit with remarkable ease. In the cool air at the top, they were all grateful for the nylon windbreakers they wore.

Mim didn't waste any time admiring the view, but strode ahead of the girls to the stone foundation of her family home. "Will you look at this!" She stood shaking her head in amazement. "So, here is where they all lived. My parents and Franklin."

"And you, too," said Corrie.

Mim hugged herself in the wind. "And where the two brothers died."

"I'm afraid that's all that's left of it," Corrie told her. She looked back to discover Jane still standing at the head of the trail. "Coming, Jane?"

"I guess." But still she didn't move. The others rejoined her.

"Is something wrong, dear?" Mim inquired worriedly.

"Not anything I can explain," Jane admitted. "It's just that, when I was here before, something happened to me. It was kind of scary. You two go ahead."

"Why don't we all just sit and rest a while?" Mim suggested. "Here. Someone has gathered some stones to use as seats around their campfire. We can wait. What's left of the old house has been here a long time. There's really no hurry, is there?"

Jane sat down and picked up a piece of burnt wood from the fire.

"Do you want to talk about it?" Mim invited, watching Jane draw charcoal squiggles on the rock.

"The first time I came up here," Jane began, without raising her eyes, "it was like Eugenie wanted to lead me to the truth."

"The truth that she could never tell me during her lifetime," Mim acknowledged softly. "Maybe you, Jane, were the one she used to find me."

"I guess she really did want you to know, in the end," said Corrie.

Mim nodded. "I shouldn't have been surprised that I dreamed of Sky Lake before I got here," she admitted. "I always said our dreams are meant to connect us. And now that I do know the truth about my family, I think Mother's spirit is at peace." She put a gentle hand over Jane's on the stick. "Don't you feel it, dear? I feel a great sense of calm, myself."

The others were looking at Jane expectantly. She smiled. "I'm okay now," she admitted. "Come on, Mim. Let's give you a tour of your house."

On the threshold, Jane hesitated once more, holding her breath, waiting for something to happen. The wind carried the scent of flowers from Mim's perfume. Nothing more. The feeling which had overcome her on her first visit did not return. It was as if Eugenie's spirit had truly gone.

Mim too lingered a moment before entering the walls of the house. "Just think," she mused, "if these stones could talk. What a story they would tell!"

"That's just what Mr. Morris said his mother used to say," Corrie remarked.

"You told me a little about Mr. Morris," Mim remembered. "Be sure to introduce him to me, won't you?" And with one hand on the waist-high wall, she took a downward step. Then something went horribly wrong. Whether Mim misjudged the distance or stepped onto a loose stone which caused her to lose her balance, she suddenly fell headlong into the foundation.

Both girls heard the snap, heard Mim's little shriek of pain. Both saw how her face drained instantly of colour. "I've broken my leg!" she gasped.

Dropping immediately to her knees, Jane felt goose bumps spring up on her flesh. There was no doubt. The sound they'd heard was the bone breaking. The girls knelt beside the stricken woman.

"Just help me get up against the wall," Mim begged through clenched teeth. She inched backwards, using her one good leg, fingers digging into the girls' arms on either side with each shift of position. Jane pulled off her jacket and put it between Mim's head and the stones. With a shuddering sigh, Mim closed her eyes.

"What are we going to do?" Corrie asked in a choked whisper.

Jane tried to remember some of the first aid training they'd had in school. "I think we have to keep her warm."

Peeling off her own windbreaker, Corrie draped it over Mim's bare legs. "What else?" she asked, her eyes darting. "I wish we had a blanket or something."

"I've got to go for help," Jane decided, standing up. "Fast. Before she goes into shock."

Corrie gulped. "You're going to leave her here, alone?"

"Of course not. You're going to stay with her. We can't carry her down to the boat. So I have to go." She looked around her desperately. "I'm going to run. It'll be faster than rowing by myself. Don't let Mim get cold, Corrie, if you can help it. And keep her awake. I think that's important too.

Keep her talking, sing to her, whatever."

"I'm really scared, Jane," Corrie admitted, her voice low, her fingers suddenly gripping the flesh on Jane's arm. "What if she, you know, faints or something?"

"That's why you need to keep her awake. You can do it, Corrie." Jane gave her friend back her hand. "I know you can. I've got to go now."

"Don't get lost," Mim croaked, without opening her eyes.

Jane knelt beside her again, wanting to touch her, but afraid of the pain she might cause. "Try to stay calm," she urged, gently. "I'm going for help, and I won't be long. It's downhill all the way. When I come to the creek...Well, Corrie can tell you which way I'll go."

Jane scrambled to her feet, and leaping up out of the foundation, she took off, running across the cap of the rock, heading east. The rock itself was ringed with sumac and Jane crashed through the thick fringe it created. Suddenly, her feet slithered out from under her and she slid down a gravelly slope, grazing the skin from both hands and her left forearm. She didn't stop to assess the damage, but pressed the heel of first one hand, then the other, to her mouth and ran on.

Now the ground levelled out again and the going was easy. Jane ran like the wind, arms and legs pumping, surprising herself at the speed with which she dodged rocks and scrubby cedars, long grass raking at her bare legs. Eugenie G. Fraser ran this way, she thought, feet pounding, brain jarring. In the night. Carrying a baby. The thought gave wings to her feet.

Ahead, the trees thickened alarmingly. Her arms up in front of her face, she broke through the underbrush and into a forest, dense with trees. The floor underfoot was damp and slippery, the sunlight filtered through a canopy of leaves. Which way? Which way? She mustn't get lost. Two people were depending on her.

Was she still headed east? How could she tell with so many trees? Jane kept moving until finally, doubt overcame her and forced her to stop. Had she somehow changed directions? Breathing hard, her heart hammering in her ears, one arm around the trunk of a poplar to support herself, she listened. She thought she'd heard voices.

Sure enough, the sound of distant laughter, a dog barking, someone shouting. She couldn't be far from the lake, then. She plunged on.

At last the trees began to thin a little and she could see a clearing ahead, but with the next step, water suddenly oozed over her runners. The terrain had been gradually sloping downward, and when she emerged from the woods she found herself at the edge of a swamp, the water black and still. As far as she could see on her left, naked trees stood amidst clumps of cat tails.

To the right, the shoreline was high and rocky, and Jane clambered up into the sunlight once more. She paused on the rocks only long enough to get her bearings. Far above her, a jet—a silent, silver speck—spun a vapour trail between the clouds.

She resumed her pace again, the thought of Mim's twisted leg and Corrie crouching terrified beside her burning in her brain. It couldn't be much farther.

Suddenly, the sound of water running. Jane pulled up sharply. Below her was a creek, too full to cross at this point. Praying it was her creek, she hurried along beside it as it rushed down towards Sky Lake. Yes! Yes, it was! Here was the pool under the willows where she and Nell had fished, and here the place where Jess had pitched his tent.

Knowing she was on familiar territory, Jane abandoned the path of the creek and reached the road before it did. Her feet met the gravel and she pelted headlong for home, the taste of iron in the back of her throat.

Finally, she burst through the back door of My Blue Heaven. Nell and Mary were not back yet, of course. Jane caught hold of the edge of the sink until her breath was restored and tried to collect her thoughts. Okay. Now what? Who to call? She had been so intent on getting back that she hadn't thought who might come to the rescue.

There was a list of emergency numbers by the phone. Hospital. Ambulance. How could an ambulance get up to the rock? Her heart still throbbing in her ears, she pressed the number for the little Red Cross hospital in McIntyre.

She was thankful for the prompt reply on the other end. The male voice was calm and reassuring, helping her to get her information across coherently. He made a quick assessment of the situation and determined that the victim would have to be lifted out by helicopter. He put Jane on hold and after a few moments came back. "Who is with the accident victim now?" he asked.

"Corrie Ottley," Jane replied, swallowing. "My friend. She's nearly fourteen. She stayed with Ms. Granger while I ran back here to my grandmother's to telephone for help."

"Okay. I want you to stay there by your phone. I'll get right back to you once help has been dispatched."

Finally, the phone rang again. Jane dropped the paper towel she had been dampening under the tap and grabbed up the receiver. "The helicopter has left Ottawa," the man with the reassuring voice said. "Everything's going to be fine. There's a landing pad here at the McIntyre hospital."

"What about my friend? She'll be all alone."

"No, she won't," the man said. "They'll take her out too, in the helicopter."

Jane sank down onto the bench under the phone, pushing her runners off one by one with the toe of the opposite foot and looking down at her reddened feet. How long, she wondered, before a helicopter could reach Sky Lake from Ottawa? She went to the front door and looked out. Nothing.

Upstairs, she hauled a clean pair of shorts and a camp shirt out of her knapsack. It seemed like a year since Corrie had stood by her bed, carefully folding all her clothing into tidy little piles ready for the suitcase, wringing promises out of Jane that if anything else exciting happened, she would call and tell her. Jess, she thought. I have to call Jess.

What was that? She jerked around. The helicopter? Jane leapt to the window. Like an answer to a prayer, Jess Howard was approaching the dock in his dad's motorboat. Jane tore down the stairs, out through the front door and down to the water, hailing him loudly, afraid he might change his mind and pull away again.

He was guiding the boat into the berth normally reserved for Nell's boat, frowning. "What's up?" he asked. "Where's your boat?"

"Still over at the rock," Jane gulped. "Mim's had

an accident. The woman I told you about? Eugenie's daughter?" The words were falling over each other. "The one who came here the other night in the storm? Corrie and I took her up on the rock this afternoon to show here where the house was, and she broke her leg."

"No kidding?" Jess lifted the motor up out of the water. "So she was the Frasers' daughter? She stopped at our place, tried to call you. Where is she now?"

"She's still up there. I left Corrie with her and came back here to phone for help."

"How come you didn't call us?"

"I needed an ambulance first," Jane explained, pushing at her untidy hair. "An air ambulance. There's one on the way. They're going to take Mim and Corrie to McIntyre, to the hospital."

"Wow, I'm impressed. It sounds like you handled everything."

"Why, did you think I'd fall apart? I had to handle it. There wasn't anyone else to do it. Nell's gone to Peterborough with Mom."

"Your mother's here too?" Jess sat back against the boat seat. "Man, a lot's been happening over here since I last saw you. So, you're just waiting till they all get back?"

"I guess so. What about you? Why did you come over?"

"No big deal," he shrugged. "I just came to see if you wanted to go for a ride in a real boat. And Corrie too, of course. But seeing as there's just you here. Then, just you. But hey, maybe you don't want to leave right now. I'd understand."

"I've been watching for the helicopter," Jane admitted. "There isn't really much I could do. I was just about to call you, when there you were. We could go over to the rock and bring Nell's boat back, if you wanted."

"Sure thing," Jess agreed, seeming happy to be given a task.

"If you just took me there," Jane assured him, "I could row it back."

"No way," Jess said. "I've got a rope. We'll tow her back."

Jane stepped down into the centre of the boat.

Suddenly, in the distance and growing louder, the sound of a helicopter beating the air. Jane sank onto the seat to watch. Once over the lake, the helicopter veered quickly to the west, in the direction of the rock. They saw it hover over the place where Corrie and Mim would be waiting. Then it disappeared from view.

Corrie won't be able to say now that nothing interesting ever happens in her life, Jane thought. At last, they saw the helicopter lift off the rock again. It headed down the lake in their direction, the whap, whap, whap of its rotors like a prehistoric bird flapping its wings. When it was almost overhead, it dipped low and turned away towards the east.

"Do you think they saw us?" Jane asked, surprised to find a sob caught in her throat.

"Hard to say," Jess admitted. He smiled, making Jane hope she would see more of that smile. "Ready to go now?" he asked.

Jane nodded. "When Nell and Mom get back we'll go to McIntyre to pick up Corrie." She spoke over her shoulder. "She's going home tomorrow. Mom's taking her back."

"What about you?" Jess asked evenly. "You going too?"

"No," said Jane. "I still have all the rest of the summer."

"Cool," said Jess, and he lowered the motor into the water.

Jane turned to face the bow, and as the waves parted in front of the boat, she felt a grin so big it made her cheeks ache.

Peggy Dymond Leavey is a writer, librarian, wife, mother and grandmother. She lives with her husband and their Labrador retriever near Trenton, Ontario. Peggy has written several books on local history, as well as many church plays and newspaper and magazine articles. *Sky Lake Summer* is her third novel for children. She has published two previous novels with Napoleon Publishing, *Help Wanted: Wednesdays Only* in 1994, and *A Circle in Time* in 1997.